INNER CHILD

MATTHEW LEDREW

INNER CHILD

CORAL BEACH CASEFILES

Published in Canada by Engen Books, St. John's, NL.

A CIP catalogue record for this book is available from Library and Archives Canada.
ISBN: 978-1-989473-16-0
Copyright © 2019 Matthew LeDrew

This book is a work of fiction. Names, characters, places and incidents are products of the author's imagination or are used fictitiously. Any resemblance to actual events or locales or persons living or dead is entirely coincidental.

Distributed by:
Engen Books
www.engenbooks.com
submissions@engenbooks.com

First mass market paperback printing: November 2011
Second mass market paperback printing: September 2019

Cover Image: Shutterstock
Cover Design: Matthew LeDrew

For
Ellen.

PROLOGUE

"Ashes, to ashes..." said Reverend Gallagher, as Mandy's casket was lowered into the ground. His arms were raised and a few flakes of snow were falling from the sky, getting caught in the same breeze that made the robes under his arms billow. He was bald except for clumps of white hair that clung stubbornly behind his ears. "And dust, to dust..."

Mandy had always loved the snow, or so Xander had recalled her once saying. Now she would never get to see it again.

"Nobody's here..." Cathy mumbled, looking around at the surprisingly small crowd gathered.

"Julie's still in the hospital," Xander said coldly, not turning away from the coffin as it landed in its hole with a dull thud. "Tommy wanted to stay with her, since her whole family was going to be here. Mike doesn't go to funerals anymore."

Cathy nodded, remembering her boyfriend's stance on the rituals of the dead.

"She was special," he said, mostly to himself.

Tears started to stream down Cathy's face. "You did everything you could."

"Sure I did," he responded, trying to hide the sarcasm in his voice.

School would start up again soon, and everything would get back to normal.

Without her.

Once again, they were forced to leave someone behind and to press forward. To commit to continuing to live, if only to honor the memories of those who could not make such commitments.

Once again, good people had died when the bad continue to live.

"It should have been me," Xander said finally, drawing Cathy's attention.

"What?"

"It should have been me. I should have been faster, smarter... or just plain ignored O'Toole. I made every wrong choice that day."

"Xander..." she sighed, crying, unable to think of a way to finish the sentence that would make him feel better.

"I have been asked by a shared friend of Mandy Peterson and I..." Reverend Gallagher continued, reaching down into his robe. "...to read a passage from the journal of Miss. Peterson."

Xander raised his head, eyes blank as he listened.

Reverend Gallagher opened the book, flipped a few pages ahead, and then went back.

Tears started to flow down Xander's cheeks.

Though she wasn't quite sure why, when Cathy saw it she cried too.

Reverend Gallagher coughed.

"There is only one passage," he said, his lower lip shaking as he, too, started to cry. "It... It is dated the night before her death. It reads simply: 'I love my life. I can't wait to live it.'"

Cathy broke down, her tears absorbed by the earth.

Reverend Gallagher stepped down, wiping his eyes in his sleeve as the rest of those gathered broke down as well.

Xander just stared down at the grave, as stone-faced as the headstone. He turned, looking up at Sara's grave on the hill, and listened.

CHAPTER ONE
AWAKENINGS

"In the darkness it followed them, just enough light for them to see. It chased them through the brush and the woods, the tree limbs scraping past them, tearing at their limbs, cutting deep, deep, everything cut deep. The wind whistled through the branches as they ran past, singing the songs of their deaths, and it was beautiful.

"It was not an evil thing that pursued them, for its need to kill went far deeper than what we mere mortals define as right and wrong. It was simply a need to be, an urge to sate the growing hunger for flesh. It did not hate them, nor they it, because they knew that it was its instinct to give chase, as much as it was theirs to run.

"The ground beneath its feet stuck to it, keeping it moist and warm; a loud sucking sound accompanying every powerful stride as it broke the twigs that sliced at its prey, its eyes never batting for fear of being prodded. It thought only of the hunt, of the taste of victory.

"The moon overhead and the ground beneath, it chased as they were chased. It ran as they did run. And as it caught them, their flesh biding mercy to its claw, they became one under a common need, a common goal, and came to know and understand each other in the hour of their passing.

"The need to go on."

⟨⟨⟩⟩

Alexander "Xander" Drew sat on the edge of his bed and stared down at the soft, carpeted floor of his bedroom. It was five-thirty in the morning and he had yet to shut his eyes, other than to blink when necessary.

He watched his hands, clasped loosely in front of him. They were shaking. They had been for the better part of an hour now, all of which he had spent looking at them and willing them not to shake. And yet, they refused to do so.

His palms were cold and sweaty, beads of moisture dripping off them down onto the floor. They were covered in scars and gaping wounds that only he could see, long since healed. In his mind's eye his wrists bled and the liquid dripping from them was a dark crimson, splashing down upon the carpet in great bursts and staining it forever. But like all things, it would heal in time. Everything here healed.

He was bare from the waist, covered in goosebumps from the harsh winter winds that made it in through his windowsill, and yet he was not cold. His body was covered in scars, too, but some of them were actually there. One was deep, still throbbing with pain every now and again, over his right side. Some that did not know him often asked if that was where his appendix had been taken out. In fact, it was where his life had been taken out, and exposed for all to see.

Other marks were invisible, like the one over his heart. He often wondered how many times a heart could be ripped out and yet still be there, still feel, still beat. Alone in the darkness, he often wished that it was gone.

His square jaw was set, his teeth clenched in determination. Every breath made his cheeks quiver and shake with frustration. His molars ground together, making a sound that even he found unpleasant, his ear lobes twitching around uncut swatches of auburn hair wet and sticky with sweat.

His eyes twitched, their blue irises fixated on his quaking fingertips. Veins had begun to form in their sclera from stress and lack of sleep. His brow furrowed, eyebrows slanting as he tried even harder to stop, and they only seemed to convulse more.

His mouth was dry and tasted of copper. He kept clacking his tongue against the roof of it and expecting to find blood, but there was none. Yet the taste remained, just like the scars.

His long nose was red from the chill, a stray drop of mucus falling from it every now and again onto his checkered flannel pajama bottoms. He responded only with an exaggerated sniff, not wanting to move away or do anything that would move his disobedient hands from view.

"Guh," he gasped finally, realizing that he had been holding his breath, his chest heaving as oxygen burned at his aching lungs.

The gaping maw of a cut on his left wrist poured out blood just as water poured from a faucet, never ending, never bringing him peace. No, never peace.

He reached down slowly with his right hand, keeping one eye trained on them on the off chance that it stopped shaking. It had not stopped shaking all the while he was in the shower, no matter how hot he had made the water. It had not stopped long enough for him to suffer down his mother's meat loaf, the fork almost falling from his trembling hands.

But maybe it would stop shaking now.

He reached under his bed and pushed aside the box of old monster comics and an unopened set of computer disks, his hand finally finding a wooden box pushed deep beneath the mattress. He clasped it firmly and pulled it out.

Across from him, against the far wall of his room, his computer monitor stared blankly at him. He had not turned it on in days, and now it stared back at him in the dark like a never-ending void. Like the abyss.

He placed the box upon his lap and ran his fingers along its smooth surface, his thumbnail catching on the frayed and splintered corners. He looked at it silently for a long moment, then lifted the cover and revealed its red velvet interior.

The light that reflected off of its contents illuminated his face, gleaming off of his eyes. It was a knife, roughly a foot long from the tip of its blade to the end of its handle. A dagger then, to be precise. It was inside a metal sheath decorated by a carving of a long line of fire, which made light sparkle and dance off of it. The flames came from the mouth of the dragon that occupied the handle, its mouth gaping open toward the blade, tail swirling down to the bottom.

His eyes darted in their sockets toward the door, making sure that it was shut tight and locked.

He picked up the blade and pressed the locking mechanism near his thumb, shifting it to the right with ease and detaching the dagger from its hilt. He placed the case back into the box gently, and then closed the lid.

On the blade itself there were markings on it that looked Cantonese but weren't, weren't anything that he could find online or in the books at school. There was blood on it already, but it was not his. No, much worse. It was the blood of someone he could not save, and it could be seen by more than just him... but he saw it everywhere, especially on his hands.

Frowning at his reflection in the steel, he turned back toward his disobedient left hand, wrist facing up.

It was already bleeding in his mind's eye.

He pressed the tip of the dagger to where he saw the cut begin in his head, slowly applying pressure until it punctured through the flesh, a small pool of blood pushing up from around it. Slowly, methodically, he traced the cut he saw with his cold steel pen, sketching out what he knew in his damned heart was right.

The blood came now in a splash as he dropped the dagger to the floor. The sound woke him, made him know that this was real and not just another illusion that his mind had created for him. This was happening, and he was strangely glad.

Pain ruptured from the open wound as the blood squirted out. Slowly, painfully, his vein filled eyes rolled back into his head. All of the colour drained from his face until he was as white as the paper that was scattered around his floor.

He clenched his teeth even harder as his body threw itself backward, slamming his head against the sloping wall of his room and falling onto his bed where his hands finally stopped shaking. The flow of redness slowed to a weak dribble, and his lungs released their final breath.

There was nothing but silence for three long minutes, as the space heater in the corner struggled to kick in and fight against the raging storm outside.

Deep inside his chest, his heart let out a final, pitiful hum as it stopped beating.

Something stirred to life in his abdomen and began to beat the second that his heart failed to do so.

His left hand twitched, ever so slightly. Then again.

It twitched and blood started to come out of it. This time his blood was a deep, thick black, and instead of flowing down and staining his dark sheets like the rest it began to flow upward against the pull of gravity, toward his fingers.

Inching along like a million ebony earthworms, growing with every pump of Xander's black heart, it slowly made its way upward.

It trickled slowly, swirling around his pinky finger and enveloping it in darkness before moving on to the ring finger, picking up speed and confidence with every square centimetre of flesh that it took as its own.

All at once, the pinky started to twitch and bend, coming back to life and exercising its right to move. Slowly, a point poked its way out of its tip and grew into a long slender talon. The black bone gleamed against the dim light in the room the same way that the blade had, reflecting the pictures in their frames that lined his computer desk. Pictures of *her*. Pictures of *them*. Pictures of those that for all his effort he could not save. And the latest...

The blackness took his entire hand, the bones in his knuckles and the joints of his fingers snapping and crackling as they snapped in two and then healed themselves simultaneously, creating new tissue and marrow to fill the gaps, making his fingers longer. The darkness met with the cut where it had originally started, and for a moment looked like a thin leather glove covering his hand before the trail continued down his arm, swirling about and picking up steam.

His elbow cracked, bending in the opposite direction, then circled around until it was upright again, twisting and ruining flesh before it was taken over by the darkness, making it look smooth again.

The ooze on his hand began to dry, crackling like the ground over the desert as the moisture left it, turning it into small, square scales.

Xander's eyes snapped open with a barely audible click, his pupils rolling back into position, only now they were larger and darker. The blue irises had disappeared, taken over completely by the pupils that now refused to reflect light of any kind. The red veins in his eyes were gone, instead becoming the same deep black that was overcoming the rest of him.

"Guh," he managed to say again. He was trying to speak, to scream out the pain and fright that came over him along with the blood. Instead blackness erupted from his lips and vomited out onto his chest and stomach, joining with the first trail and hastening its decent downward.

All of the fat remaining on his abdomen was devoured, absorbed by the beast as it pressed on, seeming to only grow in hunger with every bite it took from his flesh. His rib cage (short one rib for months now) expanded outward as the cartilage grew, as if it were going to break free of the new flesh. The ooze piled into the puddle that had been Xander's stomach, churning about and forming muscles before working its way downward.

The blackness that Xander had spewed onto his chest dug into his flesh until it reached the breast plate, wedging itself into it and spreading it apart, opening his chest as wide as possible while rising, turning the fat and existing skin tissue into brawn and sinew.

It flowed down his legs, eliminating fat there as well, replacing it with thin, sleek tone. There was a gut-wrenching crack as his kneecap shattered and his bones broke, his entire leg shaking as it bent back the other way, like a horses hind legs, then back again, moving at will like the hinge of a door caught in the wind.

His ankles disappeared, the substance from which went toward expanding the mass of each respective foot, each gaining length and becoming more pointed, perfect for jumping and leaping long distances now.

His head thrashed back and forth as the blackness traveled up his neck, flattening his hair to his skull until it looked as though there was none, circling around his head to come at his face from all sides.

The organ deep inside his right side trashed and convulsed violently, pumping as hard as it could. It wanted to win, wanted to be free more than anything else.

His eyes darted back and forth as the blackness swallowed his face whole like a giant, gaping mouth until there was nothing but the white of his eyes left, and in a moment, his pupils finished expanding, relieving him of those as well.

He stopped twitching and all was silent and still and dead. There was a short snap as his nose broke, sinking down to form a curve all the way down his face. The ooze on his head dried into the bald shadow-figure it had so many times before.

Slowly, three curved red lines drew themselves on his face, as if someone were standing over him with a pencil. The top two diagonal lines opened, revealing themselves to be red, pupil-less eyes. They stared blankly and emotionlessly into the void before it, glowing and turning upward like a cat's.

The third line opened from the bottom down, showing off two long rows of serrated yellow teeth that went further back than any human set ever did. A pinkish tongue whipped around and about, saliva dripping from it.

When it spoke its words were course and rough, its throat ripped raw from blood and stomach acid.

"Black Womb lives."

It growled, bending its knees and standing up. It looked down with those large, opaque eyes at the pool of blood on the floor, sniffing twice. It closed its mouth, and when it did it seemed to disappear into a thin straight line across its face. It turned, first with its head and long neck and then with the rest of its body, toward the window. It still whistled cold air despite the noisy protests of the space heater. It walked to the window, clutched its release with its clawed fingers, and pushed upward. Snow billowed in, the entire blizzard seeming to want to enter the room all at once.

Feeling the wind but not the cold, the creature reached out the window, dug its claws into the side of the house and scaled its way down. The window slammed shut behind it.

Carefully, it leapt to the ground and walked into the thick Maine forest behind the house. Within seconds, it had sprinted across the yard and the yard next door and was hidden by the darkness of the brush, where nothing would see it even if it were directly in front of them.

ʎ⟨ʎ

"In the shadows it caught up with them, and they did not turn away, for they found that they could not bear to fight it any longer, and more than that, did not want to.

"They came to it willingly, tired from the hunt, and felt its tingle wash over their body as its breath hit them, and they were surprised at how good it felt. How freeing it was.

"They let the monster take them whole in its passion, biting their lips as they disobeyed all that their parents had instilled in them as children.

"All for that one moment of pure, unrelenting ecstasy.

"Their bodies throbbed and convulsed with pleasure as its tongue draped over them, and from their vantage point, naked and writhing in the shadows, it could see the world of the light out of the corner of their eyes, but the world could not see them, as the darkness sank snugly inside of them.

"And even as it filled them, clouding their thoughts and their actions, their hands going places they were told never to let them go, they could not help but remind themselves how wrong it was.

"That they were bad.

"Suddenly, it began to hurt. Then more and more, until the pleasure was gone, leaving only agony and death that wrenched at their hearts, the darkness enjoying it more and more with every swell of pain that surged through them, barring its massive teeth.

"And when they died it ate them, from the bottom up.

"And all they could think was how bad they were.

"And how much they deserved it.

"And how they could not wait to do it again.

"And how it had all been worth it."

Cathy Kennessy ran her brush through her long black hair, cringing as it ripped out yet another knot. Her eyes darted to the corner of her vanity where a bottle of conditioner sat, laughing at her with its false promise of silky smooth hair free of tangles.

She frowned, then turned back to her reflection in the mirror.

It was six-thirty in the morning and most people her age were still in bed asleep, not brushing their hair and waiting for the sun to come up. But her father had accidentally woken her while he was leaving the house to go to work, and then her little sister Trina got up to get a shower and made enough noise that their mother wouldn't notice her boyfriend leaving, and then when Trina was done Cathy got in the shower, new cream rinse in hand.

Again, she cursed inwardly.

The warm water had felt so good streaming over her body, beating the dirt and the dead skin off of it. But some things didn't come off with soap.

She sat on the wooden chair she'd picked up last month at a garage sale wearing nothing but her yellow terrycloth bathrobe, gripping the handle of her brush as hard as she could. As she ripped another knot free, her robe fell open and revealed her breasts. She shut it quickly, although she was alone in the room and her door was locked tight.

She turned and looked around the room.

The only thing out of place was the bath towel she had used to wrap her hair in and the open closet door. She stared at the shadows inside the door for a long moment, then got up and walked over, retying her robe as she went. She scooped up the blue towel in one fluid motion, throwing it into the closet and slamming the door behind it.

She stopped and stared at it with her hazel eyes for a moment, one carefully plucked eyebrow arched upward, waiting for the door to respond to her gesture. Which of course, it did not.

One side of her mouth twitching in a slight frown, she forced a smile and turned back to her mirror.

Wiping the last few dabs of moisture off her pale round face, she picked up her red lipstick and pursed her small, perfect lips. Xander had given her that stick for her birthday a few months back. She remembered seeing him in the drug store looking through the wall of cosmetics with a confused look on his face, trying to pick out enough makeup to fill a small gift basket. When he finally picked out what he thought was the right shade he'd seemed so proud of himself, as though he'd accomplished something grand and spectacular. She applied it carefully, first to the bottom lip, then pressed the both of them together before leaning in and kissing the mirror, just for fun.

Slender fingers opened her jewelry box, fiddling through a jumbled mess of silver chains and charms collected from friends and relatives ever since she was old enough to wear them without strangling herself. Tapping one painted pink nail against the side of the case, she decided on a hair clip she'd gotten weeks ago while on a field trip to Los Angeles, smiling at the memory of the quirky little boutique clerk with the glasses that could have put the Hubble space telescope to shame. Parting her hair to her right side, she slid the silver clip in and snapped it tight.

She started to hum, though she did not know what or why. Music simply started flowing from her lips.

Her light, thin hands returned a few stray hairs to their rightful places. She turned, taking a quick, uncertain glance across the room again before she removed the robe, standing to let it fall to the floor before reaching over to her dresser to pick out underwear and socks.

She grunted as she slipped on her jeans, the tight ones with the frayed edges that the boys loved and her mother hated. She picked out a pink sleeveless top with frills, and as she pulled it on she could hear her boys commenting on her knack for wearing summer clothing in winter months.

She was thin and shaped like an hourglass in a way that made the opposite sex watch her intently, even those not of her age group, even when she didn't want it. Especially when she didn't want it, it seemed sometimes.

Her eyes were bright and full of zest as they turned back toward the mirror, her dark hair spinning around her as she did, accenting her facial features. Suddenly, with little to no work at all, she was beautiful.

She sighed, walking across her spacious room to her bed and letting herself fall upon it back first, looking up at the stars painted on her ceiling from the comfort of her pillows. Slowly, the smile faded from her lips. She sat up and looked around her room. The wind chimes hanging from her ceiling danced, although she didn't know where the breeze was coming from. Her dresser loomed over her, and her floor felt hot beneath her feet. It all felt so familiar, and yet something was different. Something had been made wrong that she could not make right until she knew just what it was.

Turning, she looked out her bedroom window. The snow and frost had piled up so much that she could barely even see to the street lamp on the corner. She could see only the motion, the snow blowing about outside.

She wondered if Xander or Mike were out there. If they were cold.

Sighing, she let the curtain fall back and turned back to lie down on the bed again. She closed her eyes, then let them shoot open again, looking around the room.

She did not close her eyes again until it was time to go to school.

ʌ‹ʌ

"It came at them from inside the mirror, arms reaching out with tiny mouths at the end of each and every fingertip, devouring them like tiny cannibals, so hungry that they would eat even of their own flesh.

"And when they screamed it was neither piercing nor did it render any help as blood started to pour from their gaping, open wounds, for it was a silent scream, turned inward on themselves. As the scream pierced their very souls, they stopped feeling the thousands of razor sharp teeth, and eventually all they were was the tone of the scream.

"After time, the teeth were always there. The teeth had become a part of them, hard and sharp, covering their exterior so that no one ought see them, and no one would dare touch them for fear that they, too, would be devoured.

"And without the warmth of another the teeth sank deeper and the scream grew louder. It grew until they could no longer even hear it, becoming white noise, and they became deaf to all else.

"So great was their hunger for human contact that they turned on themselves, and became the teeth, both devouring until there was nothing left.

"With nothing left to feed on, the teeth on the tips of the fingers turned to their eyes, gouging them out.

"They heard nothing.

"They saw nothing.

"They felt nothing.

"They were nothing.

"And the teeth on the tips of the fingers went back into

the mirror,

"To wait until tomorrow."

He lay on his bed, staring up at the walls around him.

The room was large, easily twice the size of the average room for a kid his age. It was lined with pictures that he had taken and that had been taken of him, of his life. That had always been a yearly ritual of Tommy Irons's. Every year, he'd change all of the pictures on his wall to those he'd taken the year before. His family had always used to call him "shutterbug" for it, back when they actually gave his actions any thought.

Most of the pictures on his wall now had been turned around, so that he would not be faced with their accusing eyes anymore.

First there was Jamie. He'd been killed. That wasn't something that happened every day back then, not like it was now. Still, that was always marked as the first. That was the point where everything turned on its head, and the simple became the sinister.

Then there was Grendel. He had betrayed all of them, but him most of all. Grendel did something horrible, then died before he ever got a chance to rectify it and make it right, as Tommy knew that he one day would have. Now he would be forever known by those that knew him best as a terrible person, which Tommy supposed was the way that it should be.

Phillips, then, for reasons that did not need explaining.

Derek, for turning on them all. For trying to kill Tommy and everyone he held dear, for no other reason than he felt like it.

Fred, his best friend, for dying.

Randy, for killing him.

Slowly, over the course of months, all of the pictures turned away from him, much in the way that the people captured upon them had.

Scattered across his bed were pins that he used to keep some of his pictures on the wall, like sensations that he used to hang his memories on.

Before him on his chest were the pictures of the newest person to have left him.

Tears dripped down his cheeks from his batting eyelids, soaking his goose down pillows as, one by one, he pinned the pictures up on the wall facing inward.

The first was of Cathy, Julie, and Mandy at the Factory. It was one of those pictures that he had taken for no occasion or reason other than the fact that he'd had his camera on him at the time and they hadn't noticed that he was standing there until it was too late. Those were the ones that he liked best, he found. Not the ones where everyone stood in a line like they were getting their driver's license photos, looking stone-drunk out of their minds with red eyes and pasty expressions, fake smiles plastered over dreary composers. No, he preferred the pictures that were natural, ones that he could look at and remember what people were like, not when they were all dressed up, but everyday normal, in case he ever forgot.

The three of them were sitting on one of the park benches that the Factory owners had bought from the city and fixed up, with an old-fashioned street lamp hanging overhead. Where they'd gotten that piece of nostalgia he'd never know, and never ask, either.

Cathy was sipping on her bottle of Cherry Coke via straw as per usual, her head turned slightly back to watch where, out of the camera's focus, Mike and James played pool. The angle made her hair drape down over a good portion of her face, turning it into something angular. She looked sexy and mysterious in an odd kind of way, wearing her tank top with the red and black vertical stripes (one shoulder strap fallen over and the other dangling) and tight jeans that left just enough to the imagination to make any man quiver.

Julie had actually managed to see him right before he pressed the shutter, but it wasn't a "deer-in-the-headlights" look. She'd been looking past him at Xander, who had just been coming in through the front doors behind him. There was a quirky smirk on her face, the one that appeared, only for a millisecond, whenever Xander walked into the room. He had been so happy when he'd developed the photos and found that he had captured it that he pinned it up while it was still wet, staining the bedspread beneath it with chemical dots that were still there now.

And Mandy. Amanda Peterson. She was doing something with her hair. Wasn't she always? She had both hands up, fixing her ponytails, inadvertently presenting her breasts through the sweater that she almost always wore, or some variation of it. There was nothing sexual about the pose, though. It was like looking at a portrait, a painting of a beautiful nude. If done right, there was nothing sexual about the nudity. That was the way this was. It was simply her in her element... her, simply being her, as no other person could. Her mouth was open to say something (most likely a sarcastic something) to Julie, who was completely oblivious to her.

Tommy had loved that picture for that exact reason. The fact that there she was, being perfect, and nobody was paying attention to her. Like a flower that bloomed only at night, when nobody could see.

Letting out a long, deep sigh, he tacked the picture back onto the wall, away from him.

He sniffed back a glob of mucus, wiping his nose in his sleeve as more tears poured down his face and shirt, tumbling to the surface until there was nothing left to them.

Hands trembling, he picked up another picture.

This one was of Cathy, Mike, Xander, and Mandy. It had been taken at the school dance just a few weeks ago, during the five minutes that Xander and Julie had been together. They were all sitting on a line of chairs against the wall. Usually he despised photo opportunities like this, but this one was natural enough.

Cathy wasn't herself, though. She was sitting three chairs away from everybody else, looking away from them, too. Still, there was that mystery about her, only accented by the fact that she wasn't part of the group in this shot. One of her hoop earrings had captured the light from the flash, giving her a movie star quality.

Mike just looked sad. Not upset per say, just plain not happy. His golden head of hair seemed a little less shiny, somehow. His head was down, tilted just slightly toward Cathy, who was not returning his gaze by any means. His hands were clasped in front of him, and even though it was a photo, you could just tell that he was twiddling his thumbs.

Xander was smiling.

Tommy had been very glad he had gotten a picture of it, for he was sure that he would need proof of this monumental event.

Xander was leaning side-on against the chair, his arm draped over the side as he talked with his hands to Mandy, as he was prone to doing when he was actually in a good mood. It was a rare occurrence.

And Mandy. Again, she looked so pretty. It was like she was trying hard to look plain and just couldn't do it. It made her shine all the more brightly in the darkened gymnasium. Her shoulder-length brown hair was pulled back behind her ears, revealing the m-shaped scar on her forehead that she was usually so self-conscious about, but now she was relaxed enough that she wasn't thinking about it enough to hide it. And those eyes. Those big, green eyes that always sparkled, even when there was no light for them to reflect.

A tear fell, plopping against the photo-paper with a tiny splash.

He pinned the picture back.

When he picked up the final picture, his lower lip started to tremble. This was the one he had been dreading, when there was nothing else to catch his eye, to distract his attention. It was Mandy Peterson. She'd been captured from the waist up, turning to look at him after he'd called out to her from behind. Her hair was dancing around her in swirls as she turned, her eyes wide with that sparkle he'd been talking about. He'd taken this just a few days before it had happened. Her lips were pale and he found a great deal of peace in them, just a little bit of her teeth showing. She'd gotten so mad at him for taking that picture, caught in a classic Peterson fury and nearly slapping the camera out of his hands before starting to laugh at the goofy, weak expression that had adorned his face.

Slowly, he turned, pinning that one on the wall, too.

Sniffing back hard, he turned into his pillow and closed his eyes, hoping to cry himself to sleep and get at least a few moments rest before his alarm went off.

He would not.

 ⋏⟨⋏

"They did not run, for they did not wish to. Instead they stayed there, bathed in light as the darkness swirled around them, taking each breath long and deep, just in case it was their last.

"The beast circled them, clacking its nails against the ground, making them twitch as the suspense rose to a nearly tactile level of unbearableness.

"It was maddening.

"At first, they did nothing. Then, all at once, they turned about and lashed out, pounding their fists into the creature, sending it scampering away, laughing at their attempts.

"That they would try to harm that which they simply did not understand, such being the plight of all mortals.

"But the blow missed, of course, and the arm traveled around the curvature of the earth, picking up speed as it went, until finally, they hit themselves.

"And the blow that would start to harm others

"Would cause their suicide."

"Argh!" Mike Harris screamed, punching the concrete wall in front of him. His knuckles were abound with an odd confluence of sensations, cold from the snow and wind that churned all around him, but at the same time warm thanks to the blood that flowed freely from them.

He heard the satisfying crack as something within his wrist popped free, smiling in contentment as it did. Blood from open wounds splattered in star shapes from the spot where he hit, while fresh ones were being torn open.

"Are you okay?" Came a voice from behind him.

He hit the wall once more, letting his hand linger there, using it to prop him up as he turned to look over his shoulder at whoever had spoken the kind words.

It was a short black man, bundled up in a parka with a hood, staring out at Mike from beneath its shadow. A scarf hung loosely around his neck, billowing in the stiff breeze that seemed as though it wanted to touch everything near it in some way, shape, or form. The man's hands were buried deep within his pockets, and he looked to be shivering. He took a step closer to Mike, taking a hand out of his pocket and reaching it out. "You're not hurt, are you?"

Mike stared at the man through squinted eyes for a long moment, the snow sticking to his hair and eyelashes, then he turned around to face the wall again, drawing back to punch. He grunted as saliva sprayed from his mouth and hit the ground, freezing there.

"Or something," he growled, deep in his throat.

The man shook his head and kept walking.

"They looked deep inside themselves,

"And they realized that the darkness had been inside of them the entire time.

"Following them like a shadow."

CHAPTER TWO
TEE YOU VEE

"Fuck," Cara cursed, as the Factory's heavy metal door caught a gust of wind and slammed her in the arm.

The Factory had always been a staple of life in Coral Beach, and in many ways it changed as society within the township changed. In recent years it had become a local arcade/club/pool hall where many of the town's teens went when they had nothing else to do, which was frequently, especially if they had a mind to stay out of trouble. When it came to legal fun in Coral Beach, the Factory had long been the be-all and end-all. It jutted up out of the otherwise calm Northeast landscape, always loud and exciting and neon.

Cara had been working there for three weeks now, even since Paul Russ had gotten sick with pneumonia and quit in a huff when he realized that he'd opted out of health benefits in order to help save up for a new car. In a town like this you didn't interview for a job. When Paul quit the owner called Cara and said that she knew that Cara had been without work for some time, and if she wanted to work there. Cara had hastily agreed.

The work was hard, but she didn't mind. Most nights she went home with her hands bleached white from the cleanser they used on the floor and her throat burning with the stuff, but one hot shower was all it ever took to reset her back to normal. Her husband liked having the extra money that her employment was bringing in, and they hadn't fought at all since she'd started. They'd even discussed taking a vacation together in the spring.

She only found two downsides so far: the stench of dope that she had to contend with every time Calla Mc-Fadden spent more than ten minutes in the bathroom, and the abuse that her left arm was taking.

Every day when she took the garbage out back to be picked up the next day, the back door managed to slam against her. With her arms full of trash bags filled to the brim with paper cups and soda cans, she never had any defense when it slammed against her full force, always into the meat of her forearm. It had happened so many times in the past few weeks that the flesh there was tender to the touch at all times, the large cluster of bruises there going beyond the normal colours of black and blue and delving into much scarier purples and reds and an odd, jaundice yellow that frightened her. Women began to look at her as though she'd been abused (even though Steve had never so much as raised a hand to her), and she felt that the more she protested this the more they thought it was true.

She threw the large black bag in her right hand over the guardrail and into the dumpster, grunting with exertion as she did. She heard something glass inside it break when it hit, but paid it no attention. Sweat dotted her brow just above her eyebrows and the undersides of her arms felt the chill of the cold Maine air as she grabbed the second bag and tried to lift it, failing the first time but succeeding the second.

He watched her from the trees just beyond the dumpster, his breathing picking up speed as he watched her sweat-laden bosom heave its way almost clean out of her shirt as she dropped the second bag into the dumpster.

Her apron got tangled in the guardrail and she pulled it free, spitting a large glob of saliva out onto the frozen concrete steps before heading back toward the door.

She stopped in the archway, her ears perking up as she swore she heard something behind her. She turned around and saw the same forest that was always there... same evergreens that had randomly grown all around the back wall of the building, each one weighted down with pounds upon pounds of fresh snow until they looked like they were about to crack off. The pure white of the virgin powder made the shadows between them seem even darker though, and she couldn't see anything that was going on between the branches.

He smiled as she looked right at him but didn't see him. She had green eyes... he loved women with green eyes.

She stared out into the trees, focusing in on one rock that stuck up out of the snow near the tree line (which was nowhere close to where he was watching her from) and could not shake the feeling that there were eyes on her... that same feeling that kept her from getting changed in public washrooms even where there was nobody around, or go swimming in anything more revealing than a one-piece.

-Chic.-

There was a sound, like something she'd heard before but could not quite place... almost like the way her dog's nails sounded against the hardwood floors when they needed to be cut. She paused once more, staring at a spot just to the left of where she had before... then turned to step back into the Factory.

He arose, emerging from the bushes with a thick scowl on his face and started forward.

Cara let the door to the Factory close behind her, careful not to let it slam into her behind when she left as it had on more than one occasion.

He bolted forward, making his way for the rusted green metal box that she'd thrown the trash into.

Sven Douglas was a small, middle-aged man with very little hair and buckteeth. What hair he did have left was graying in uneven clumps around his ears. He hadn't washed in days, and looked like it.

He'd been living on the streets for two days now, ever since he'd first gotten wind that somebody was hunting down all the Tees. At first he didn't believe it, and when he heard exactly what people said had been hunting them, he believed it less and less. Still, the first day after Mandy Peterson's funeral four of their senior members had been brought in by the police, and that wasn't something that he could just ignore, so he moved out onto the streets to give whoever was after him less of a chance of finding him.

-Chic.-

He'd managed to get two good meals out of his bank accounts before the police froze them, and then it had finally occurred to him: not only had most of his compatriots been brought into custody, but at least one of them must have rolled on him. He'd been hungry all day yesterday, and now it had finally come to this... feasting on trash when he would have much preferred to have been feasting on the trash lady.

Eyes glued to the door as he approached the dumpster, he turned toward the back of the building and stared out into the space beyond. There was a small sliver of street visible to him from here, and if he could see out than that meant others could see in.

-Cllus.-

Sweat began to pour down his brow and his throat started to ache with thirst as he remembered all of the times he'd seen kids finish half a bottle of Coke and then screw the top back on and throw it out. He could almost taste it even now, flat and warm but still so good.

Careful to avoid a sharp spike of metal along the dumpster's edge, he pried his thumb under the ledge and threw it open.

A shadow came out so quick and was so fast that Sven barely had enough time to scream before he was on the ground, pinned there at the shoulders with large, powerful hands. He shrieked, in such a high voice that he didn't recognize it as his own. He didn't know who that person screaming was, but he knew one thing for sure: whoever they were, they were going to die.

As he watched, horrified, the shadowman seemed to grow eyes and a long, slender mouth that glowed dark red. It came down so far that it was hard to tell where its mouth ended and its chest began, but somehow Sven knew that it didn't matter. This thing was all mouth.

Deep inside the skin of the Black Womb, Xander smirked to himself. What that contortion of muscle and tissue translated to on the face of the Womb was nothing short of horrific, a wide-angled grin with hundreds of sharpened teeth, pointed cheeks curving to block small sections of those large, triangular eyes. One of his arms was pulled back, the palm open and fingers outstretched; the claws at the tip of each extended to their fullest length.

Right then, that smile was all that Sven could see. The eyes, the black skin, the claws... that was fine. He'd been told about all of that before, although he'd never actually seen it. It was the smile that truly bothered him, making his sweat run and his blood boil over with fear as his heart raced within his chest.

The whole area smelled like cheap marijuana, and it only increased every time Sven exhaled. All of Xander's favourite land marks behind the building had been covered in snow to the point that he did not know one thing from another, and even in the fresh snow, the ground was littered profusely with cigarette butts.

Sven's eyes were bloodshot beyond comprehension, both from the fear and the drugs. His hands shook as they tried to pry away the Womb's arm to little effect, and his teeth rattled about inside his skull.

He was cold, too cold to have just come out. A few strong whiffs with his senses-heightened nose confirmed Xander's suspicion that Sven had been staying out here from quite a few days, trying to hide from the cops, the snow... and of course, from him.

"Do you have any idea how happy I am to see you?" Xander asked rhetorically. In his head, the words sounded enough like his own. But when they came out of the Womb's mouth, they became ridged and slurred and hoarse, like someone with the worst case of strep throat in history. He often wondered what the Womb sounded like when it was in complete control... but he could hardly ever remember those escapades, and even if he could, the Womb was ninety percent mute anyway.

Sven did not speak in return, even though Xander had given him pause in which to do so. He did, however, mutter a brief prayer to his mother, never once taking his eyes off that smile.

"A part of me blames myself for never trying this sooner. I guess I'll never know exactly how many lives I could have saved if I had actually put my all into hunting you guys down." He sighed, swiping his claws forward gently but accurately, stripping away the clothing on Sven's right arm until it was bare, save for a few strands of fabric. Exposed on the biceps was a broad, red letter T, though it was tattered by scar tissue and many recent removal attempts.

"I thought so," Xander sneered, the Womb's smile growing ever so slightly in its perturbed nature. "Looks like you tried to get rid of it. Naughty, naughty. You should have known I wouldn't forget a face like yours anyway."

He lashed out, rending his talons across Sven's face, loosening flesh from muscle and sending blood streaming down.

"Not anymore, in any case," he added, cocking his head to the side as he retracted the claws, punching Sven once in the central plexus and then again in the stomach. Sven bent over in pain and Xander ended the brief scuffle with a sharp blow to the back of his head, sending him face first into the snowdrift.

He sighed, turned to walk over to where he knew the Old Sitting Stone was located and brushed the snow off it. He sat down, leaned one arm against his knee, and let out a long breath that sent condensation billowing out in front of him.

Three days. That was all it had taken to round up the last of the living Tees and bring them to justice. For four months he had been fighting them, and now the last of them had finally gone down for the count.

He growled inwardly, turning and slamming on the back door to the Factory, hoping to get Cara's attention so that she would find the fugitive. He turned and began walking into the woods, slowly disappearing as morning light peeked over the hills.

CHAPTER THREE
FEAR ITSELF

-BEEP-
-BEEP-
-BEEP-
-BEEP-BEEP-
-BEEP-
-BEEP-
-BEEP-

That sound had kept Julie Peterson awake all night. She stared out of the window of her hospital room at the snow being blown off the roof, swirling gently to the ground, sparking in dawn's first light.

The room was mostly white and sterile, a stark difference from the clutter and colour that she was used to. There was one window in her single room that shone light in on her, its trim an off-white that was one of the more grabbing contrasts in shade in the place. The sheets that covered her looked and felt like paper. The only bit of colour in the room was a pegboard filled with get-well cards reserved for her well-wishers. There were precious few there, but a few homemade ones from her friends had brightened her demeanor ever so slightly. At some point during the night, a nurse had rearranged the machinery used to keep tabs on Julie's vital signs, and her heart monitor now completely blocked the pegboard.

She stared up at the slow drip of the IV with bloodshot eyes as each drop hung, suspended for an instant, before dropping into the tube that took it into her veins. Her eyes were bloodshot and watery, their pupils milky and unfocused, and her mouth had dry cracks at the corners.

Her usually carefully placed brunette hair was a tattered, static-filled mess. On any other day she might have been worried about it, even going into fits trying to tame the wilder strands, but today she could not care less.

There were dots of a white, vomit-like substance stuck to the corners of her mouth, and a bad taste had been growing exponentially in the back of her throat for the last two days.

Her tanned, freckled face had become pale and sickly, her infectious smile driven far away.

She had been dressed in a backless paper robe with two drawstrings on the back that became unbearably uncomfortable every ten minutes or so. As it was, fabric was bunched between the gown and the flesh on her back that threatened to pinch very soon, forcing her to move. She arched her backside ever so slightly to remove the discomfort, and pain immediately shot through her, starting from a burning hole in her chest and smoldering up her spine and into her brain, exploding there and sending tiny embers of agony sprinkling violently down through her body until her limbs twitched uncontrollably. Her teeth clenched as the heart monitor escalated its assault on her ears.

-BEEP - BEEP-
-BEEP - BEEP-
-BEEP - BEEP - BEEEP-

It punctuated her pain perfectly, like a tiny mono-syllabic narrator, each tone marking the anguish that pumped throughout her via her veins. The agony slowly subsided as she settled back down into the bed, the pinch of her skin against the paper gown minuscule in compari-son. Her lungs heaved in despair as the scar tissue around them stretched the bruises there, letting tiny slivers of fresh blood out of her body.

She quivered, trying for only a moment to halt the shaking of her lips and the batting of her eyelashes.

On the front of her gown, in nearly the center between her breasts, a small spot of blood wetted the paper. She noticed it immediately, worrying for a moment that it would continue to grow, but to her relief, it ceased.

Days ago, although in many ways it seemed like months, Julie Peterson had been shot trying to save her young cousin, Amanda.

Sven had managed to get his handgun out, and Julie was now wrestling with him for control of it, the both of them roll-ing around in the snow, biting and punching at one another for control over the weapon.

BANG!

All heads turned, wondering where the shot had come from.

Sven turned, the gun now visible in his hand, as well as the fountain of blood streaming out of the gaping maw in Julie's chest.

"No!" Tommy screamed.

Mike slammed Langley into the frozen ground and they both ran toward her. Cathy turned the corner and saw what was happening, and all three of them bolted toward Sven, who dropped the gun in fright as both men pounced on him. Cathy went to Julie's side.

"Julie!" Cathy screamed, pulling the girl's hair out of her face and being very careful not to touch the wound. "Julie, are you all right?"

"Don't..." she tried to say, as blood gurgled up from her throat. "Don't stop. You have to find her."

The bullet had managed to miss all her major organs, coming extremely close to her left lung. It hadn't gone through-and-through, but almost. It became lodged under the skin of her back, just to the left of her spine. Upon awakening from the operation, the doctor had told her that she was lucky.

If she had been able to speak or move at that time, she may have assaulted him.

Lucky would have been not getting shot.

Lucky would be Mandy still being alive.

Lucky would be not living in Coral Beach.

The pain subsided, and the scarring and stitches around her wound settled back into place. Slowly, the heart monitor regained its usual, annoying chime.

Something moved quickly in the corner of her eye.

She turned swiftly, her damp sweaty hair flailing about as she turned to face whatever it was. There was nothing but the corridors and the white walls.

She heard something squirm right beside her. As she turned to see, her chest objected to the motion by sending coarse pain through her fragile form. She stopped moving, letting her eyes dart about inside of her head again, looking for the source of the sound that now seemed to be coming from all around her... the floors, the walls, the curtains... it was even in the pine fresh scent that hung on the air. Suddenly, everything was quiet again, except for the steadily increasing tone of her heart monitor.

-BEEP-

-BEEP- BEEP- BEEP-

-BEEP- BEEP- BEEP - BEEP-

She looked around at every corner of the room that she could see from where she lay, inspecting every shadow until she was absolutely certain that she was alone in the room. She let out a long sigh of relief, her chest heaving once as she did. Grinning at her own insipid paranoia she turned onto her side, the pain only stinging for a moment as she did.

Her scream was heard in the nurse's quarters two floors down and seven rooms to the right, even before her heart monitor could alert them to the emergency.

CHAPTER FOUR
ETERNAL

The school bells chimed rhythmically, a hint of the tune that had once been apparent still lingering. Four years ago when it had gotten a wealth of new funding from the board after years of learning how to tighten their belts, the school had been faced with a surplus. At the end of the year they had been faced with two choices: either spend the surplus three thousand dollars by the last day of classes, or have that remaining money cut from the following year's budget. After a few hasty ideas were thrown around, the school administration finally decided on a digital bell to replace the old mechanical ones that still hung above the doorway to every classroom. For a few years the song they played (a midi riff of the school's theme, which itself was taken from an old Irish folk diddy) rang out at a lively tempo, but the speakers were old now and the sound mostly came out as one streaming blurb, like a tone-deaf man trying to sing in harmony with the birds outside his window.

"Damn," Xander cursed, craning his neck around the corner to see a gaggle of his classmates slowly drift their way into Coral Beach High. He sighed, then turned back quickly before one of the teachers noticed him.

"What have you got first period?" Mike asked, nursing his knuckles gingerly. He carefully peeled back a tiny strip of loosened flesh until it was almost off, then brought it to his mouth and bit it clean, spitting out the sour, copper-flavored remains.

"Tech. Barrett," Xander said glumly, taking a long haul of his cigarette and then throwing it to the ground with the rest of his growing collection. "You?"

"Physics. Mr. Calender," he replied. He was scuffing the dirty snow at his feet without really thinking about it, letting large piles of the fluffy white get onto his sneakers and soak in until his toes were freezing. "Any luck last night?"

"Finished off the last one outside the Factory in the wee hours."

"Oh." Mike nodded. "That's good, right?"

Xander's face twitched in disapproval. "Went down easy, didn't put up any fight at all. Sometimes I wish I could turn off the enhanced agility and all the other bullshit. I'd like to have had a real go at him."

"It's not all it's cracked up to be."

"So I'm told."

Mike again brought his hand to his mouth, sucking on the blood that was slowly ebbing out of the wound, his lips making an odd smacking sound as he did. "Any word?"

There was a sound emitting from deep within Xander's throat, as he reached for his pack of smokes, then decided against it, remembering the annoying chime of the homeroom bell.

"I'll take that as a no," Mike said.

"I'm going to go see her today, after class," Xander admitted, biting a stray end off one nail.

"Hmm. That's good, I'll bet she'll like that."

"They wouldn't let me in before now."

"Bastards. Is this a... private engagement?"

Xander turned toward his friend, making eye contact finally. "I was going to ask."

"Say no more," he offered, brushing it aside with his hand. "Me and Cathy are there, as long as you need us to be."

"Tommy, too," Xander added, getting up and brushing snow from his rear.

Mike shot him a look.

"Guy really proved himself back there. He deserves to be kept in the loop as much as we can afford."

Mike nodded slowly, then motioned for the both of them to start toward their classes.

Xander gave him a curt nod. He took one step and slipped in the snow, twirling as he tried to catch himself and twisting his ankle, landing on his back with his feet perched in the air. "Fuck!" He cursed loudly, attracting the attention of the few remaining students in the courtyard. "Fuck. Fuck, fuck, fuck."

Mike smiled, offering his friend a helpful hand. "Enhanced agility, huh?" He grinned, pulling Xander to his feet.

"It's been a long week."

"Right."

"Shut up."

"I agreed with you."

"Is this your idea of shutting up?"

"What did I say?"

"Because if it is... let me tell you, you do not have what is known as a firm grip on the idea."

"I said nothing."

"Keep it that way."

Mike snickered, as the two of them lumbered off to class, Xander limping a little as they did.

᚛ᚁ᚜

Chanelle McDonald's sky blue eyes darted over the colourful wall in front of her, a heart monitor beside her beeping silently. It was a special, noiseless model used only in the children's ward. The wall was a tapestry of colour and flavour, decals of various children's characters covering it, some of them with stethoscopes and blood pressure pumps. Mickey was there, and so were Bert, Ernie, and Blue. They all smiled down upon her, the morning light reflecting off the whites of their eyes and teeth, making them eerie and creepy.

Her plump face was mushed against her paper pillow as she heard the sound again, a sick slithering sound that reminding her of the snake from the *Jungle Book* movie that her little brother always watched, over and over again, no matter how many times she begged him to put on one of the other dozens of movies that her parents had accumulated for them over the years. She shut her eyes as tightly as she could, praying that it would go away. That it wouldn't happen again, not to her, not to any of them. Not again.

Her brunette hair was in tangles, matted by sleepless

nights in the stale, rough sheets.

Somebody started to scream, then stopped.

There was a muffled sound, and a high-pitched whine. It sounded like when her father's car wouldn't start.

The room got colder somehow, as Chanelle tried to find a way to close her eyes even tighter.

Bed sheets started to rustle, and there was the sound of kicking and pounding... then suddenly, there was nothing. After a moment of silence, she opened her eyes again. The eyes and smiles of the decals no longer were aglow with the evanescence of sunlight. She stared at Mickey, concentrating on the gold buttons of his overalls for a moment. There was a sneered laugh as the shadow moved, accompanied by the slithering sound again, slowly fading away until the door closed.

She shuddered deep within herself as she listened intently to the quiet that was wrapped all around her like a blanket.

"D - E - A - T - H. Death," Miss Waller read aloud as she wrote each letter in big, bold letters across the chalkboard. The white chalk between her fingers scraped against the board and pierced the ears of every student in the classroom (including Cathy Kennessy, who was sat in the seat closest to the window).

Tabitha Waller had been the Family Education teacher at Coral Beach High for just over ten years now, ever since she'd transferred over from Kannibus regional. She was in her mid-forties but looked as though she were in her late sixties, with wrinkles that made either side of her face sag like melting wax and short hair that she had curled every Wednesday with the rest of the golden girls at the Luxury Discount Salon. She claimed to have moved to help take care of her brother who was ill with lupus, but she'd really been shunned out of town when the liberal core of Kannibus, Maine found out about her secret life. Tabitha Waller was a lesbian, one of only three she'd been able to detect within the limits of the town. The other two were a couple (the Forges) living as sisters. Tabitha hadn't had a date the entire time she'd lived there, and the Forges had begun to joke that if she didn't get one soon she'd be forced to turn in her "Rainbow Pass."

The change to Coral Beach had been sudden and jarring, but she'd gotten used to it here. After a few months she learned that Coral Beach, for all its right-wing sensibilities, had a prospering gay district, if one knew where to look. There was a bar near the center of town that held a ladies night on Tuesday evenings, and it hadn't taken her long to figure out that the ladies who frequented were of just her sort. She found that she could be happy here. No matter how bad the town had gotten in the past few months, she decided that neither hell nor high water was going to chase her out of another community... not while the students kept paying attention during her sex ed lectures and body shots on Tuesdays remained $3.99.

She turned toward her class, her features curling up into a smile. The wrinkles of her cheeks made deep shadows on either side of her lips, framing them there as if they were needed to hold her smile in place.

"Death. We deal with it every day," she said, turning around to face her class and finding that almost all of them had their eyes glued to her or what she'd written on the board. She allowed herself a smile, then swallowed and moved into the brunt of her lecture. "It can be found in literature as recent as the newest Stephen King novel or as far back as the first printed book, when Cain killed his brother Abel in Genesis. Shakespeare also used it more than his fair share, might I add. It is found in our newspapers, our plays, movies, and television... there has been a strong case made against its influence in the video game world on impressionable youth... and death is in our homes. Family, friends, loved ones... they all go eventually. But there are many ways to deal with death. Can anyone think of an example?"

The classroom was stone silent, as students tersely avoided eye contact with one another and fiddled with their erasers or tapped their pencils against their notebooks, waiting (if nothing else) for Miss Waller to answer her own question.

She looked out across her students, hands on her hips and her wrinkled face fighting the urge to curl at the corners. "I believe that there is no 'wrong' way to deal with death, that it is specific to each individual person. However, I think that death is also one of life's great learning tools. I think that if we do not get better at learning from death and learning from how we react to it, then we might as well resign ourselves to death as well."

There was a sound from the audience from the far wall.

Waller looked up and smiled, scanning the row for a student that would meet her eye. "Did someone have something to say?" she asked, in a voice that was neither encouraging nor stifling.

Nobody in the class spoke, only exchanged glances, many of them directed toward the middle window.

"If somebody has something to say..." the teacher trailed off, finally focusing the climax of many of the students' looks on one person in particular. "... Miss Kennessy?"

Cathy looked up from her notebook, suddenly aware that the majority of the waking eyes in the room were on her, including the teacher's. "Nothing," she said finally, her eyes immediately going back to her paper. "I didn't say anything."

"If it's worth saying at all, it's worth sharing with the rest of the class, Miss Kennessy." Waller smirked, leaning in as if to listen to what Cathy had to say.

Cathy slammed her pencil down on the desk, her eyes meeting the teacher's for the first time and revealing them to be so filled with anger that they were getting misty and lipid at the corners. "I said 'yeah, right,' okay?" She snapped, spittle flying from her lower lip. Stopping herself, she turned toward the window and tried to focus on the snow-covered elm sitting outside. She couldn't even really see it though, her mind tumbling with angry thoughts as her cheeks got redder and redder, unable to stop the onslaught of aggression.

Miss Waller stepped back a pace, her eyes widening. "Um..." she stammered, then finally composed herself. "If you don't agree with my lecture, then you are more than welcome to voice your own opinion on the matter, as all of my students are."

Cathy let out a heaving sigh and rolled her eyes.

"Miss Kennessy?"

"Okay," Cathy huffed, her voice almost giddy with rage as her arms flopped down onto her desk. "There are no wrong ways to deal with death? That is the biggest load of fucking shit I have ever heard."

"Now, Miss Kennessy..."

"No!" Cathy interjected. "Cursing at you is how I'm choosing to deal with death right now, so by your own philosophy, you can deal with it. And 'learn from death?' 'Oh, it all has a lesson?' Screw off! A week ago... *one week ago*... a thirteen year old girl was raped and shot! Not in New York, not in L.A., here! As in, down the street, here! And now you're standing around talking about what we can learn from it? Tell you what: as soon as people can start learning not to kill and maim each other, I'll get on finding out what I can learn from death, you fucking old 'tard."

"Miss Kennessy," Waller fumed, her nostrils flaring. "You can either apologize right now for your actions and tone, or you can see yourself to the--"

"I wouldn't stay another minute," she snapped, cutting off the teacher as she scooped up her notebook and headed for the door.

She paused at the doorframe for one final instant and shot a disgusted glare at Waller then slammed the door behind her, sending a plaque hung not far from it crashing to the floor.

‹‹›

Mandy Peterson walked down the hall, her brown shoulder-length hair bobbing around her playfully as she did. Her big, green eyes lit up the hallway as her smooth, chubby cheeks grew wide in a grin as she caught sight of her friends.

"Hi guys!" She chimed musically as she waved high above her head, bouncing a little on the balls of her feet as she did. She was wearing a blue Coral Beach Cougars team sweater that flopped about aimlessly on her as she moved, making her look larger than she was.

Xander looked over at her and smiled, showing all of his teeth. His eyes lit up as she entered the room, coming over to join him, Cathy, Mike, and Julie around the cafeteria table.

"Hey, you!" He chirped.

"Hey yourself!" She replied, spreading out her arms and allowing herself to fall back onto the table with a big, dopey grin on her face.

Xander laughed.

"I think you get cuter every time I lay eyes on you," he said. He closed his eyes theatrically, and then opened them again with a shocked expression. "See? I was right! You're more beautiful than you were a moment ago!"

"Stop it!" She chuckled, slapping him on the arm with her notebook. "You're so corny, Xander!"

"That's Alex," Julie corrected, turning away from her conversation with Cathy and slowly putting her arm around him, giving him a kiss on the cheek as they spooned. "And I don't think he's corny at all. I think he's cute."

"Cute?" Xander said, raising an eyebrow.

"Dude..." Mike laughed out loud, punching his friend on the shoulder as he put his arms around his own girlfriend. "...You got the cute. You are officially lamer than you have ever been in your life."

"Shut up," Cathy groaned, grabbing his face with her thumb and forefinger so that his lips stuck out like a fishes. "I haven't heard you say stuff like that to me in months. Even if I did, you'd have to be *upgraded* to cute to get out of the doghouse you're in."

"Oh yeah?" He smiled, reaching out and tickling her furiously.

"Oh my God! Stop it, Mike! Stop it!" She squealed, laughter roaring out of her until her sides hurt.

Xander laughed at them, then turned back to Mandy. "So, what are you doing tonight? Anything?"

"Yeah, Mandy," Mike reciprocated, turning toward her while still tickling Cathy. "What are you doing tonight?"

"Well," she smiled, her rosy red cheeks blossoming with vibrancy. "I was think maybe I'd--"

"...cosign and tangent. These formulae give us what our chemical charts will be at both points C and F, respectively."

Xander looked around, realizing that he was, and had always been, in Mr. Howards' last period Chem class. He glanced around, making sure that nobody had noticed him as he had zoned out, then tried his best to catch up on his notes from Gwen Watson in front of him.

"The graph will always be the same at both points C and F when you are presenting chemicals with at least three sodium ions in its formulae, as you can see in the following three examples..."

Xander stopped, carefully placed his pen down on his desk, and watched his fingers as they moved.

Scars.

CHAPTER FIVE
REPRISE

"Hi! Sorry you got near-fatally shot in the chest! Here, have a fruit basket!" Mike said, holding the basket before him at the hospital gift shop. "Yeah, that's convincing."

"Well, sure, if you say it like that," Cathy groaned, taking a bite out of her chocolate bar. "How about... 'Here are some fruit, but I guess you had enough of that with Xander?'"

Mike shot her a look, then turned back to the pitiful fruit basket (consisting mostly of bananas) and placed it back on the shelf. "I swear to god, this is the most depressing room in this hospital."

"The gift shop?"

"Yeah. Full of cheesy things and useless junk. When I was sick that time, all the stuff my parents bought me just made it worse. It's like all the happy face balloons and shit have become symbols for sickness. Whenever I look at them now, I get all depressed."

"Hm," Cathy grunted, poking at a stuffed teddy bear with 'get well soon' sewn into its heart-shaped stomach.

"I find it to be an interesting part of human subculture."

Again, Mike shot her a look.

"What?"

"No more Discovery Channel for you," he said flatly.

She rolled her eyes. "Come on, we have to find something."

"You pick. Girls are impossible to shop for anyway."

"Oh, really?" She smirked, placing a hand on one hip.

"Well, yeah," he said positively, picking up a fluffy heart pillow and waving it before him. "With girls there is so much to choose from, so many different tastes. With guys, it's simple: give him and comic book featuring women who have such big breasts and are so skinny that in real life their backs would be broken. That's all. You're done. He's happy... and you can read it before you even give it to him and he'll never know, so you're happy too."

Cathy stood, arms crossed, looking at him with one eyebrow cocked. "What girls?"

"Huh?"

"The comics. What girls in the comics?"

Mike chuckled to himself, putting down the heart pillow that he had, until this point, still been waving. "When you do this about regular girls it's weird enough. Fictional girls boarders on psychotic."

"What. Girls."

He sighed, hanging his head as low as it would without injuring his neck. "Rogue. I like Rogue, from X-Men. The comic, not the movies."

"There," she chimed, patting him twice on the head. "Now was that so hard?"

"More than you will ever know."

"I like Scarlet Witch from the Avengers."

Mike's head shot back up, looking at her bug-eyed.

"It's the tiara," she giggled, scrunching up the bridge of her nose.

Mike shook his head in amazement, turning back toward the shelves.

"Look at that!" He almost yelled, pointing with both hands at a small teddy bear wearing an eye patch, a cast and a crutch. There was even an adhesive strip across its bum. "Seriously, is that necessary? That's really depressing to me. 'Hey kids, your stuffed animals can get sick and die too!'"

"I'm sure that's the message they're trying to portray there, lover."

"Bears are stupid anyway," he grumbled.

"I like bears."

"You would."

"What's that?"

"Nothing, my sweet darling baby girl," he sang, smiling at her.

Rolling her eyes, she let her hands slump to her sides in frustration at the gift buying process, then turned to face Mike in her exasperation.

"Chocolates," they both said in unison.

ʎ✗ʎ

Xander and Tommy both sat on the couch in the hallway outside Julie's room. Both men sat forward in their seats, elbows leaned against their knees and hands clasped together before them. Tommy looked at the wall opposite them, filled with pictures of children that had been lost and children that had been saved. The previous far outweighed the latter, a notion that made him want to look away, yet he did not.

Xander's head stayed turned in the direction of Julie's door without actually looking at it, his right knee shaking violently. He made no effort to stop or even control it.

"You know, you can go in," Tommy offered, motioning toward the door. "I'll stay here and wait for Mike and Cathy, if you want."

Xander smiled, turning his head down and away from the door. "Naw," he said, nodding at Tommy in appreciation. "I wouldn't know what to say if I went in there alone."

Tommy gave him a knowing look, nodding. "How about: 'how are you?' or 'I missed you?'"

Xander snorted. "Or, 'Hey, since you got shot not long after and I didn't have a chance to ask, are we still broken up?'"

"Right," Tommy agreed, pouting a lip. "Yeah, that one I'd leave out."

"You think? I thought it might make for an alright ice-breaker. Maybe after I could bring up that zit that was coming out on her back the last time we made out. See if it got any bigger."

"More topics to steer away from," Tommy laughed, tapping Xander on the knee with his fist. "I think... I think maybe this is supposed to get easier."

"No," Xander whispered, looking down at his hands. For a moment, he could have sworn that there was blood on them. Drenching them. "It's supposed to get harder."

"Hey!" Cathy said, jogging up the hall with a shopping bag full of chocolates bouncing against her side as she went.

"Hey," Xander said, getting up and accepting her hug as she reached him, rubbing his hands soothingly over her back. He turned to Mike then, who gave him a nod as Cathy turned and gave Tommy a hug as he rose to greet her.

"What did you guys get?" Mike asked, holding up his own bag full of assorted chocolates.

Xander and Tommy both reached into their bags, each pulling out a small, stuffed bear with a broken arm and a crutch.

There was a long pause as Mike stared blankly at both of the bears, then at the faces of the men holding them.

"Looks cute," he said finally, dropping the chocolate back into the bag and turning toward the door.

Down the hall, a nurse wheeled a bed with a long cloth draped over it out of a room and down the hall toward them.

All four of them faced the door at different angles, each trying to look as casual as possible in their inability to open it.

"Are they giving her meds?" Cathy asked finally, taking a turn looking at all three of her men. "Does... does anybody know if they're giving her any meds?"

Xander bit his lip.

"Um, yeah," Tommy answered, coughing a little. "Yeah, her Mom... Sam?... She said they'd been giving her Morphine and stuff. For the pain."

"No, for the cookies," Mike said under his breath. No

sooner were the words out of his mouth than he shot an apologetic look at Tommy.

Tommy forced a smile back.

The nurse continued to wheel the gurney down the hall toward them. One of the legs was loose and kept trying to pull the cart to the right, making a high-pitched squeaking noise as it did.

"No comments like that when we get in there, please," Xander said without looking at anyone in particular.

The three of them nodded, neither one looking at the other, as Xander took another step forward toward the door. Suddenly, his nostrils flared. He turned, a sickened look on his face as the nurse wheeled the bed past.

Cathy, Mike, and Tommy turned as well.

Hanging out from over the edge of the bed, barely uncovered by the sheet, was a small, chubby hand. It was as white as paper. The nails on the end of each finger were tiny and blue.

Cathy turned, burying her head into Mike's arms.

All of the colour drained from Tommy's face, and he brought a hand to his mouth.

Xander frowned as he turned back toward the door and sighed. He reached out, grasped the knob, and turned it.

CHAPTER SIX
VISITING HOURS

Xander opened the door and Mandy smiled up at him from beside Julie's bed, her lopsided grin slowly fading to an expression of worry and remorse. The look did not suit her face, making the whole scene appear wrong somehow.

"How is she?" Xander said, taking quick steps to be by her side as he took off his jacket and laid it over Julie's motionless feet. He took her hand and rubbed it softly as Mike, Cathy, and Tommy quietly came in behind him. Mike took an extra pace to give Mandy a simple kiss hello on the forehead, and then sat down next to Cathy.

"She's doing better," Mandy admitted, taking hold of Xander's hand as he held Julie's. "The doctors say that all the bleeding's stopped, finally. She could wake up any time, but... sometimes these things take awhile."

Xander nodded, giving her a quick smile. He reached up and pushed her hair back behind her ears.

"You've got such a pretty face," he chided, poking her softly on her nose. "I don't know why you'd ever want to hide it."

She rolled her eyes. "It's not my face I'm trying to hide. It's this big ugly scar."

Xander smiled, then he turned to Julie.

"Do you think she can hear us?" Tommy asked nervously, cracking his knuckles every few seconds. He never once took his eyes off Julie. "I mean, can she understand?"

"I think so," Mike smiled.

"Yeah, I read somewhere that talking to them can help." Cathy nodded. She tried to recall the magazine, then decided it was unimportant.

"Julie," Xander coaxed, squeezing his girlfriend's hand tighter. "Julie, you have to wake up, okay? We need you to wake up now." He paused.

Nothing.

"Jules, come on," Mandy coaxed, leaning in. "You gotta wake up. I love you, Cousin. You gotta wake up."

Julie's eyelids fluttered.

Xander smiled, large and bright.

"Julie!" He said louder, trying desperately to get a response. "Julie!"

Slowly, her eyelids opened, a smile prying around the corners of her mouth as she turned her head weakly to look at Xander.

"Alex..." she said, her voice painful to even hear. "... Alex, I love

Xander opened the door, revealing the cold, sterile room that seemed to have been sealed from within, like pickles inside an unopened jar. At first, all that was visible were dual lumps where Julie's feet poked up near the end of the bed; then, as each of them entered the room and came around the corner, she came fully into view.

She looked pale, almost as white as the walls that surrounded her. She stared straight up and the stucco ceiling until all four of them were almost on top of her. She jumped a little when she finally noticed them, clenching her chest as pain shot through it, then quickly faded.

"Hey," Xander said softly, sitting on the corner on the bed with both his hands on his lap.

"Hey," she replied, sniffling as she pressed a button on a remote that brought her bed into a sitting position. She winced a little when it stopped. "You guys came."

"Yeah," he said, reaching out and taking her hand finally, which she made no motion to stop. "Yeah, this is the soonest they'd let us in."

There was a long silence that was almost palpable.

"Um... I got you this," Tommy said finally, breaking the quiet as he reached into his bag and pulled out the stuffed bear with a broken arm.

"Oh, yeah," Xander said, having forgotten, pulling out his bear, with the crutch. "Me, too."

"Thanks," she said sweetly, putting one on each side of her, smiling at them both.

"We brought chocolate," Mike said between bites, motioning to both him and Cathy. Cathy grabbed the bag from him, putting it beside Julie.

"Thanks," she said honestly, staring down at the bag hungrily. "These are so gone the second they tell me I can eat solid foods."

Cathy smiled weirdly. "Sorry, didn't think."

"It's okay," she sighed, playing with a tuft of hair on

the head of the bear Xander gave her. Her eyes turned away then, staring at the far corner of the room.

Again, Xander's nostrils flared and his brow furrowed. He turned to Cathy, who gave him a confused look, and he back.

"How... are you?" Tommy asked finally.

"The pain is less," she said, still looking at that spot in the corner for whatever reason. "The drugs they got me on make me kinda wonky, though."

She turned quickly, as if she had heard something behind her, hurting her chest again.

"How so?" Mike asked, tilting his head.

She laughed. "Earlier today I thought there was something in the room with me... It was horrible. A nurse had to come in and give me something to calm me down."

"If it's little pink elephants or Smurf porn, I know what you're talking about," Mike smirked, drawing glances from everyone. "What? You can't tell me I'm the only person here who's ever hallucinated about Smurfs getting busy?"

"No..." Julie interjected, shaking her head. "It was... I don't know what it was."

"Can you describe it?" Xander asked finally, squeezing her hand.

She took it away from him. "It was big. It was really big... tall, I mean. But it was really thin. And it didn't have any eyes... just big, black holes. It was wearing a suit..."

"A suit?" Xander questioned, raising an eyebrow.

"Yeah, but it didn't have any skin. It was all muscled, no skin anywhere that I could see. And it had this big bulge in its pants. It was grabbing itself and coming toward me and it said something, then I screamed and it went away."

"What did it say?" Cathy asked, cuddled into Mike now.

"It said... You have nothing to fear, but fear myself," she said distantly, shivering even though it had not gotten any colder in the room.

"Hn," Mike grunted.

Her brow wrinkled, sweat dotting along it and along the neckline of her blouse.

"It's okay," Xander said, in the softest voice he was capable of. "It's not important."

"Yeah. Yeah, I guess," she said faintly, then turned to the group as a whole. "Thank you guys so much for coming... but, would you mind leaving the two of us alone for a while, please?"

"Sure," Xander said respectfully, turning to the others. "Um, if you guys wanna stick around I'll probably only be a-"

"No, Alex," Julie said softly, cutting him off. "I meant... could you guys leave me and Tommy alone?"

Xander turned toward her as Tommy moved in and knelt down by her bed. She grasped his hand and squeezed it tightly.

"Yeah," he said finally, realizing that she hadn't even really heard his response, as he, Mike and Cathy walked out the door.

"Dr. Marx?" Nurse Williams called, opening the door to his office even as she knocked on it.

Dennis Marx dropped the notepad he was looking at, his knee coming up off the floor and slamming into one of the sharp corners of his desk. He cursed, frustrated, and ran his hands through his balding salt-and-pepper hair as Williams entered the room.

"Bad time?"

"What do you *want*, Debra?"

She swallowed. Her name was not Debra, but she was not about to correct him. He was a stubby little man that looked like a caricature of a mole, with large rimmed glasses and a small nose that came to a sharp point an inch or so in front of his face. There was an actual mole growing out the side of his neck, which was large with rough edges and hairs growing out of it that he refused to get looked at.

"The blue baby in room three eighty-one got dealt with, she's fine. Mr. Douglas is stable with non-life threatening wounds, and there was a code in Mr. Adams's room. We lost him."

"That's good," he said, already reabsorbed in his notepad.

She stared at him, tilting her head to one side.

"I mean, not *good*," he sighed, looking up from his papers. His hands were out in front of him as though he were pleading with her, his red Bic pen still clasped in his left one. "It's not good, it's... thank you for telling me."

Williams nodded, then turned to leave. The office was cluttered, with papers strewn everywhere containing mortician reports, medical journals and tox screens compiled over months and arranged in no particular order. There was a large stack of patient files on a love seat in the corner that had toppled over and intermingled with one another like a shuffled deck of cards, and she did not envy whoever had to rearrange them when it came time.

There was a mini-fridge in the corner with a padlock on it. It was the first time she'd ever seen it there, and her eyes lingered on it for a moment.

"Is there anything else?" Marx barked, looking up from his notebook and realizing she was still there.

"No..." she replied, shaking off her temporary daze and smiling at him. "Not at all, Doctor."

She let herself out and closed the door behind her.

He watched the door for a full minute, as though expecting it to do something else. When he felt secure that we was alone again, he walked over and locked it with the small latch near its knob, then fished his keys out of his pocket as he made his way over to his fridge.

He consulted his notes for a moment, then hunched over and pulled out a long tray full of glass vials, each one sealed tight with a taped-on label written in his own illegible hand. He lifted a few out, read their contents, then shoved them back in. On the fourth try he found the one he was looking for, smiled, and placed the rest of the tray back into his cooler.

It was labeled anthrax.

ʎⱱ

Xander sighed, flopping down on a chair one hall down from Julie's room.

"That's the last time I'm nice to that guy," he grumbled, slouching as far as he could without falling off the chair.

"Oh, stop whining," Cathy berated, giving him a little kick to the shin. "She just wants to thank him for saving her, is all."

"Oh, I'm sorry. Stopping Adam Genblade and defeating all of Circe doesn't qualify as saving anymore. I may have saved the whole town, which she is in, but does anybody say-"

"Are you done?"

"Very," he said, sucking in his lip and sitting up quickly.

"Good."

"So, what now?" Mike asked, frowning as he leaned up against the wall with his arm over his head.

Xander sighed, turning back to Julie's room and staring at it for a long moment.

"You guys can go on home," he said finally, dragging his hand through his hair. "I'm gonna stay here. Just in case she needs something."

Cathy stepped forward and hugged him, then she and Mike walked past him and out of sight.

Xander leaned his face forward onto the balls of his palms let out a deep, sorrowful sigh.

CHAPTER SEVEN
OMENS

Jillian was an Aegean cat, and there was absolutely nothing wrong with that.

That was what her master, Josie, had said to her often. Josie would rub her back or scratch behind her ears and say "Jillian is an Aegean cat, and there's nothing wrong with that with that," sometimes over and over again. Jillian, for her part, would close her eyes and purr ecstatically.

Three months ago Jillian had gotten out and had met a young stallion without a name, and now she was so plump that she could barely walk without waddling from side to side. Josie had been almost giddy when she'd discovered that there would soon be a litter of cute little kittens running around her home, and Jillian had taken to lounging about and enjoying herself in the sun while she waited for the big day (not that she had been opposed to doing that before she'd gotten pregnant). Then a week ago, she'd gotten the irresistible urge to get out... She wasn't running away, no, she'd definitely go back. She knew that Josie would worry without her. But she knew she had to find somewhere else to go to have her kittens.

She'd spent the last week in the hospital basement, curled up amongst a pile of old rags very near the furnace. Although she wasn't as good a mouser as she had been when Josie had adopted her from her previous home in the shelter, she'd still managed to make a good living for herself on the mice that lived in the ducts and walls leading to the hospital kitchen. The staff did not know who to thank for their pest control, but they were thankful all the same.

A door opened somewhere that shone a long stream of light over the basement. Her eyes went wide, glowing as they turned toward its source, but she did not move. There was an old janitor that came down here once every few hours, and although he'd never noticed her she'd become adjusted to his presence. The door closed again and the light vanished, but there was still something there... she could feel it even if she could not see it.

She listened hard, and for a moment all she could hear was the faint drips of the leaky pipes leading into the sewage system. After a moment she heard footsteps coming toward her. There was nothing sneaky or mysterious about them. They clambered and clunked on the cold concrete floor, and Jillian was convinced she could see them now, moving in and out of the little light offered from underneath the stairwell door.

Her ears flattened back and she hissed.

CHAPTER EIGHT
DOWN DEEP

Xander leaned forward on the hard green plastic chair because the curve of its lumbar support had been digging so far into his back that he was convinced no human spine could withstand it. The door to Julie's room remained at the far right of his field of vision. It had not budged since he left it over an hour ago. Nobody had gone in, and nobody had come out.

He sighed and ran his fingers through his hair, then slapped his hands down onto his jeans and rubbed along the ridges in the denim, letting out a long huff of air.

The nurse's station was at the end of the hall. There was a large, big breasted woman standing behind the counter there trying to complete some paperwork who stopped to say hello to every person that passed, even people that did not say hello to her or acknowledge her in any way. As more and more people passed she became more and more agitated, pressing down on her pen so hard that it started to cut through the paper.

A short, stumpy doctor passed by. She looked up from

her work and said, "Hello."

He nodded in return.

She went back to her work, taking a moment to find her place again.

A patient walked by. She looked up from her work and said, "Hello."

The patient rolled his eyes and continued to the bathroom.

A young man wearing a striped shirt and carrying one of those bandaged bears walked by. She looked up from her work and said, "Hello."

He didn't even respond, or notice that she had spoken to him.

She went back to her work each time increasingly frustrated.

Xander shook his head and forced himself to look away. When he did, Julie's door came into view again, immediately coming into focus as though it had been waiting for him, like some trickster hiding behind a corner ready to leap out a yell boo at a moment's notice.

"Why don't you just go in?"

"It's not that simple," he replied. "She asked me to go."

"Then why don't you leave?"

He did not respond to that, keeping his eyes glued on the door.

Several long moments passed, and he felt a lump grow in his stomach. It was like his entire body was trying to collapse in on itself through a black hole in his chest. He felt every part of him slowly moving toward it, his shoulders slumping forward and his knees coming up. His head felt heavy, though he was not tired. Every part of him felt raw, and he wanted to claw at his chest with his fingers to try and dig the feeling out.

He heard something behind him, the solid *ticktack ticktack* of something crawling inside the wall or in an air duct. He felt like it was on him, whatever it was, and for a moment when he looked between his legs he could have sworn he saw a mouse scampering over his foot. He jumped slightly, realizing it was just his shoelace.

"Fuck," he breathed, reaching down and tying the errant lace. Sweat had begun to bead his face and all his joints felt stiff.

There was a loud rattling sound, and he got up from the chair and turned around. There was a large duct behind him spitting out air and sounds. Beyond the grate was dark, but he could see the edges of what looked to be a destroyed paper-wasp nest. He shivered, and then turned back toward the door.

"Fuck this," he huffed, patting his hands against his jeans again but this time coming back with a battered cigarette pack in his hand. He fumbled with the top and pulled one out. It was soggy and limp and he put it behind his ear and started down the hall toward the exit.

The big-breasted nurse looked up from her work as he passed by her station, a fake smile plastered on her chubby face. "Hell--"

"You have OCD," he snapped, continuing down the hall without even looking at her.

She stared, dumbfounded, then shrugged and went back to her work until the next person walked by.

⋏⋌⋏

Cathy sat in Mike's den on an old couch with holes in it, the sponge that poked up through them oddly comfortable. She'd been here before, but not often. The room had been limited to being his father's office for years while he'd been working from home, but now they were free to use it as they wished. His mother still never went in, not because there was anything sensitive inside, but simply because years of having to stay out had ingrained itself into her subconscious to the point that she often forgot the room was even there.

The room did not match any other in the home. A few years ago Mike's mother had gone on a redecorating and remodeling kick that had left most of the house open concept and in shades of bright greens and subtle yellow hues. This room (which had been all but forgotten in her projects) looked like the rest of the home used to: muted earth tones and hardwood everything. Hardwood floors, hardwood furniture, even the heavy curtains had been bought to be the colour of the hardwood, though they had since faded into a grayer version of it. Mike used the room a lot, much as he did now, sitting at the computer desk and staring into the screen.

She watched him intently for some time without even realizing it, her mind drifting from one thought to the next. "You know, until recently I didn't even realize your house had a computer."

He paused, then turned around and looked at her with a raised eyebrow. "Of course we have a computer. What house *doesn't* have a computer?"

"My house doesn't."

He paused and thought for a moment. "Huh."

He shrugged, then turned back to the monitor.

She sighed, then got up and moved over to the bookshelf and started going through the titles, running her fingers along the spines as she went and kicking up dust.

"Your dad sure does like James Patterson," she said, counting each book in her head.

"Nobody's perfect," he mumbled. The computer made a soft clicking sound as a new window opened.

"What're you doing over there, anyway?"

"I am looking up who the Mets are starting next season."

She turned around from the bookcase and shot him a weird look, one eyebrow arched and both lids bulging. It was wasted on his backside. Had he seen it he would have shot coffee out of his nose. "You like baseball?"

He turned in her direction only slightly, then motioned toward the wall that the desk was up against. It was filled with pictures of a young blonde boy in a baseball uniform resting a bat on his shoulder. Some were designed to look like large baseball cards (with actual stats and awards typed along the border) and others were black-and-white team shots in which the boy was clearly identifiable by his hair, which looked almost paper-white in them.

"Oh my god, that's you!" She smiled, walking over and tilting one of the frames to see it better.

"Of course it's me. Who did you think it was?"

"I don't know. Your cousin. I don't know."

"I don't have any cousins. You know I don't have any cousins."

"You're so *cute*," she said, ignoring him. Her tone was

the same one that he'd noticed her using on children, her voice raising several octaves until it sounded like it could shatter glass. "Where's this one?"

He leaned back on his chair to see what she was referred to. It was a picture of him at about ten standing on a long row of bleachers. His father was towering over him, having to lean down so that his head could be in the shot and still get all of Mike. Mike was wearing a stripped Mets uniform and cap, and they were both holding up Mets flags. Mike's face was covered in freckles that were much darker than they were now.

"That is me and my Dad at a Mets game."

"You went to New York?"

"No," he laughed. "The Mets came to Boston to play the Red Sox... I've never been to New York. I wish."

She smirked. "You went to a Red Sox home game dressed like that? They must have loved you."

"I'm sure." He smiled, then turned back to the computer and clicked the mouse again.

ᚲᚩᚷ

The basement door closed behind Xander and he was in the dark again.

That was okay. He found that he'd always liked the dark, even as a child. There was something about a black room that made him feel safe... as though he was curled up tight in a warm blanket so snug that no light could get in.

The basement was not warm though. It was so cold that gooseflesh covered his arms and made his hairs stand on end.

He stood at the top of the stairway that led down to the basement and waited for his eyes to adjust. After a moment when they did not, he sighed and reached deep into his pants pocket and withdrew a metal butane lighter. He popped the top and flicked the flint three times before it finally caught, illuminating the narrow stairwell in dull oranges and deep, black shadows. He held the flame back behind his head for a moment and tried to see where he was going. The shadows made the already narrow stairs look even thinner than they were. They seemed to sway back and forth as the light flickered in the slow breeze of the drafty basement, winding this way and that until they finally reached the concrete below.

He took his cigarette out from behind his ear, wet from sweat around its tip, and pinned it between his lips. Bringing the flame to his face he took three puffs in rapid succession, then pulled back and checked to make sure the cherry was lit. It ebbed at him like a dull red eye sticking out of the darkness, and did not fade. He put the butt between his lips and took a long drag, closing his eyes blissfully. He could feel the smoke in his neck and chest, the way the heat made him feel whole. He held it as long as he could and then let it go, the smoke playing and dancing with the flame and casting swirling shadows on the wall.

There was a sign on the wall next to him. He raised his lighter, and found it to be a No Smoking sign. He smirked, then turned his attention back down the stairwell.

It had stopped winding back and forth, although the flame still flickered about. There was a cool breeze coming from the cracks in the concrete that was still making him shiver. Every time he thought he was getting used to it the wind outside howled again and he heard it whistle through the cracks an instant before it touched his skin like a dead arm.

He narrowed his eyes, took another short puff of his smoke, and started down the stairs.

⋏⟨⟩⋏

"So, that's everything?" Tommy asked, glancing at Julie then looking down at his hands again, rubbing his aching knuckles.

"Yeah, pretty much," she replied, her eyes dancing about in her head, as if searching her mind for any strands of information that she had forgotten. "Yeah, that's it."

He stopped for a second to mull things over.

"That's quite a bit."

"Yeah, pretty much," she repeated, trying hard to flatten the wrinkles out of her blankets.

Again, Tommy remained silent.

Julie's eyes shot downward, not knowing from his reaction whether or not to be ashamed by what she had told him.

"I had no idea that all of that happened," he admitted, almost sorely. "How come nobody tells me anything, anyway?"

She grinned. "It's not just you. Everyone's really secretive here. I think it's something that they put in the water, y'know?"

Tommy smiled a little at that. "Yes, actually. Everyone here has their own plans, their own little agenda. Julian, Derek..."

"Phillips, Randy..."

"Xander, Mike..."

"You." She grinned, raising her eyebrow at him.

He looked as though he were about to continue with another set of names, then stopped and smirked at her. "You catch a lot more than people give you credit for, don't you, Miss Peterson?"

"I try," she replied coyly. She turned from him to pound at her pillow, trying to get it comfortable.

"So, what about you?" He asked, leaning forward. "Hiding any other demons?"

"No," she said quietly, in a matter-of-fact tone of voice. "None of my demons are metaphorical."

ᚷ

The basement seemed to go on forever.

Xander took another puff of his cigarette and let the smoke curl around his head like a wreath. It stung at his eyes and made them water but he didn't care. With one hand holding the lighter high, he needed the other in case he fell.

The flame was almost useless. It seemed to get swallowed by the darkness just over a foot in either direction, devoured by the drafty cold of the hospital basement. He turned around just a few feet from the bottom of the staircase and found that he couldn't even see it anymore.

What was worse was the smell. He couldn't smell anything down here except the sterile stench of disinfectant and bleach that wafted down from the air ducts and was pooled in little puddles of chemicals that whoever spilled them thought would dry but never would down here. It blocked all his senses and made him helpless as he took one slow, deliberate step after another, making sure that he wasn't about to trip over a barrel or some stray tube.

Something sucked in the distance, like the last bit of water draining down a sink. Every few seconds there was a different sound of water gushing through one of the insulated copper pipes as somebody, somewhere in the hospital turned their faucets on and off. It never came from the same direction twice, sometimes so far and faint that he had to strain to hear it and sometimes right above his head. It shot fast as though it might burst, then slowed down to the barest dribble in an instant.

That tight feeling built in his chest again, like his body wanted him to try and touch his toes with his shoulders. He took another puff of his smoke and moved on.

There was a skittering in the darkness, like thousands of tiny legs all moving in unison along the floor. Without even thinking about it, his mind conjured up the image of a giant centipede with long pincers in the front crawling along the basement floor toward him, so big that it could wrap all around him like a boa constrictor before devouring him whole, all the while hearing that skittering clicking clacking as he went down the creature's gullet.

He shook the thought off.

"Nng," he snarled, as he took another puff and the ember reached his calloused fingertips. He brought the burn up into the light and watched as the blister slowly faded away until it was gone completely, like watching an artist erase a mistake he'd made on the page.

Holding the dwindling smoke between his lips, he reached into his pocket and pulled the pack out again. Of the two left he took the straighter one and clasped it between his lips on the other side of his mouth. Even though his lighter was already out, he lit the new smoke off the cherry of the old one (again puffing three times to make sure it was going) then flicked the old butt into the darkness.

It traveled far, much further than he would have thought he could flick it. It spun end over end long into the darkness, finally striking off a steel pipe and tailspinning its way down to the ground, casting a small circle of light around it as it went.

Right before it went out, there was something between Xander and the light... a black figure that stood tall and lanky, with its legs stretching out like poles. Its shoulders were hunched over, and although Xander could only see the outline of its form, he could tell that it was looking at him.

The ember went out, covering the distance in the blanket of darkness again.

Fear gripped at his gut, sticking into his stomach at all sides like a clawed hand.

"Hello?" He called, holding up his lighter and squinting into the darkness.

There was no reply, except the skittering of thousands of tiny feet again.

"Is somebody down there?"

Again, there was no response.

Casting a quick glance back in the direction of the stairwell (even though it had long since faded into the darkness), he started toward where he's shot the cigarette.

Several pipes gushed water overhead at once, and he heard at least one toilet flush. A furnace cut in somewhere to his right, and that slurping sound like water being sucked down a drain continued. So did the skittering. It got louder and louder the further into the basement he went.

Without touching it, he took a long drag from his smoke and shot the exhale out through both nostrils, traveling down behind either side of him like a dragon.

The flame still only allowed him to see a few feet in front of his face, and was dwindling.

He stepped in something cold and wet and knelt down, putting two fingers from his free hand down into it. He brought his hand into the view of the fire. At first he thought it was rusted water, but then the stench of ammonia (already prevalent here) shot into him and slammed harshly into his sinuses, and he realized it was urine.

He wiped his hand in his jeans feverishly.

The furnace cut in again and almost made him jump out of his skin. It was right behind him.

"Jesus," he cursed, holding out the flame as far as he could and seeing the tall metal sphere that seemed to go all the way up to the ceiling.

There was blood spattered across it in an upward arch.

Again he felt that pang deep inside his abdomen, almost like hunger or a nicotine fit but not either of those things. He stepped forward slowly and brought the lighter down until the soft orange glow found the carcass of a black-and-white Aegean cat.

Blood had matted into its soft fur and made it course and sticky, especially around its stomach. It was fat and looked as though it had been pregnant, and Xander found himself making a small, pitiful sound that he usually would have associated with something Cathy would do.

Her tiny face was bent upward, her eyes and mouth frozen open in fear and hatred. Her tiny, sharp teeth still had spit on them.

She had a long gash going from her pelvis to her neck, exposing her organs and her plump, full uterus. One of her legs was missing.

Xander shivered.

There was a collar around her neck, and he reached out carefully to turn its tag toward him.

It read: Jillian.

A pipe above him gushed water again, and there was that slow sucking sound... followed by a wet smacking.

His brow furrowed and he turned around, raising the lighter high again and taking several determined, brave steps into the darkness until the light found the wall.

There, huddled in the corner, was a man in a deep black suit.

His back was turned to Xander, but he could see the back of his bald head and the wisps of hair that clung to it in uneven clumps. The flesh on his skull was not smooth and round like his father's; it was scaly and segmented into long lines like stringy bits of muscle still clinging to the bone. It was huddled over something against the wall, completely oblivious to Xander and the light that now bathed it. He moved back and forth slightly, like a chair left to rock in the wind.

The suit looked pressed and clean, like the ones his grandfather had worn to church every Sunday until the day he'd died. It also looked like the suit they'd buried him in. It was too short on this fellow though, revealing thin legs and nonexistent ankles sticking out from underneath them.

The sucking sound was louder here, and consistently followed by the wet slap of flesh he'd heard a moment ago.

"What're you doing?" Xander asked finally, still standing a few feet from it.

It spun around quickly, and Xander froze in place.

It had no eyes. Just like Julie had said, it had no eyes... just black holes that seemed to go on forever like the basement. The light caught nothing in them. It had no flesh either, just malformed muscle that squirmed about like worms all over its face. It had a long nose and sharp, yellow teeth that could be seen right until they disappeared into his gums because it had no lips.

There was blood and flesh caught between its teeth.

It howled at Xander then disappeared, scurrying off into the darkness faster than even he could see. The scuttling centipede feet he'd heard all along was deafening now, skittering off along the wall away from him.

"Fuck!" Xander yelled, dropping the lighter.

It fell to the ground and snapped shut, leaving him in darkness.

He dove to the ground and patted for it, his cigarette falling from his lips and rolling along the floor.

His hand connected with something wet and slimy and he pulled it back, screaming. Finally he found the lighter and fumbled with it for a moment before realizing he had it upside down, turned it over, and lit it.

Light again invaded the basement, and he let out a

long breath.

Holding the light forward, he saw what his hand had come to rest on.

It was Jillian's missing leg.

He shuddered, wiping his hand in his pants again and chasing along the wall after the creature.

It seemed as though he were jogging forever, much longer than he would have said the width of the hospital could have been. He'd lost all track of where the stairwell would be and didn't care.

Finally, he came up to the other wall and stopped. The skittering was gone, and so was the creature. He looked all around, but all he saw was darkness.

"Fuck!" He yelled, kicking the wall violently.

It rang. Like a bell.

He turned and saw an air duct near the corner, two feet wide and one foot high. There was a grate covering it that was screwed on, and the darkness inside was only made deeper by the flame in his hand, just like the one upstairs.

He stared at it for a long moment, the gong that his kick had made echoing down it until it disappeared.

Slowly, he bent down and lowered the flame to see inside.

He screamed louder than he ever had when its arm came through the grate and clawed at his face.

CHAPTER NINE
TIMOR

The phone rang in three different places in the Harris house: one in the kitchen, one in the living room, and one in the den. Each had their own separate and unique rings that were annoying enough on their own, but when they all combined together at different paces and volumes they instantly brought migraines with them.

RIIIING!

Doo doop doo doop doo doo doo doop!

Braaaaang!

It did this three times before Cathy tilted her head away from Mike's, forcing their lips apart. They were lying on the old couch in the den with one of Mike's feet caught in its sponge-stuffed holes and Cathy's legs wrapped around Mike's midsection.

"Are you going to get that?" She asked, even as he tried to lean into her lips again.

"I hadn't planned on it, no."

"Come on, it could be important."

"Not more important than this, I guarantee."

She shot him a look.

"Fine," he smiled. She opened her legs to let him go and he hopped on one foot over to his father's desk, snatching the cordless phone off its cradle and bringing it to his ear. "This had better be good."

"It's real," Xander said into the hospital payphone he held clutched between his cheek and his shoulder, dabbing white fluffy gauze against the other side of his face as he did. It stung violently, but he didn't flinch away.

Static roared in Mike's ear and he pulled back, wincing. "Who is this?"

"Shut up. It's real; I need you guys to look some stuff up for me. I'm going to stay here and try to see what's going on."

"Is that Xander?" Cathy asked, sitting up on the couch and adjusting her shirt.

"I think so, but he's being a douchebag," Mike grumbled, making no effort to block the receiver as he spoke. "What's real?"

"The thing Julie was talking about," Xander huffed, pulling the gauze back from his face and examining the level of fresh blood on it. He leaned to the side of the phone and examined himself in its metal back. There were still four white lines down right side of his face where its claws had run, but the wounds were closed. "The Fear thing. It's real."

"Real?"

"Real. I need you to find out what it is and what it can do, if you can. I'm hoping I can just cut it to bits and be done with it, but the fucker's fast. It's not human. It could be like me or Black Heart or something. Either way, we have to find it before it can do any damage to Julie or anyone else."

There was silence on the other end of the line.

Mike pressed the receiver against his chest and looked at Cathy. "He's finally lost it."

"I can hear you."

"I didn't say anything."

"I have superhuman senses. You can go fuck yourself. What's the problem?"

Mike frowned. "I'm sorry, I'd assumed we weren't going to be chasing after figments of your ex-girlfriend's imagination today. But then again, I took my crazy pills this morning...did you?"

"It's real."

"One sec, I don't think Cathy believes me," Mike said, pressing the speaker button on the phone and then resting it on the cradle again. "Can you hear me?"

"Yes, I can hear you."

"Good. Now, be a dear and tell Cathy how batshit you've gone."

"It's real. The Fear demon thing Julie was talking about. It's real."

"Real how?" Cathy frowned, stepping a pace toward the speaker as though it were really Xander in front on her.

"Real as in I'm-looking-at-the-cuts-it-made-across-my-face-right-now real."

Mike stopped smiling. He turned white. "Did you fall asleep? It wouldn't be the first time someone in our group saw something otherworldly in a fever dream."

"Exactly," Cathy said. "Some of us relive past experiences, some of us dream up dead assassins, Julie's head makes up monsters... and some of us picture pornographic blue midgets."

Mike shot her a look.

"I wasn't dreaming. I was smoking."

"You said you'd quit!" Cathy huffed.

"Big picture, please," he barked into the phone, drawing the attention of the fat nurse at the station again. "You guys couldn't smell the fear on her, all right? Give me a little credit."

"That bad?"

"It was like the city dump at the town of fear. Whole room reeked of it."

There was a silence.

"What do we do?" Mike said finally, clearing his throat.

"Go to the library and see if you can find anything. I don't even know where you'd start. It eats animals, but something tells me humans are on the menu, too. I want to deal with this fast."

"Is it that you want to deal with this, or that you don't want to deal with anything else?" Cathy asked.

"Whatever. Same difference." He paused when he heard something behind him. A nurse (not the big one with OCD) wheeled another gurney out of the pediatric ward. The body on it was covered over with a sheet, but it was clear it was no more than three feet long. Xander turned and watched it in silence until it was around the corner and on its way down to the morgue. "Shit."

"What?" Mike asked, already pulling his coat on. "What is it?"

"It's the kids," he said, his voice almost a whisper. "It's killing the kids."

He hung up the phone without another word.

Mike and Cathy exchanged glances, then headed for the door.

CHAPTER TEN
CTPAX

Xander marched down the hall, trying hard to soften his clenched knuckles before he got to the pink and ba-by-blue door of the pediatric ward. His eyes squinted as the door got closer, the same stench he'd come across in the basement becoming more and more potent with each breath he took. It was the stench of death, and it was com-ing from a child's bed.

Fuming, he placed his palm flat against the door to shove it open, then stopped.

He sighed, stared at the back of his hand, and then hung his head.

"Not so easy, is it?" Mandy asked, walking up beside him holding her hands behind her back. She looked down from his hand to his shoes theatrically, mimicking his own actions.

"You shouldn't be here," he grunted, still staring at his boots.

"Why?" She asked, in a voice much like that of a child who was the only person not picked to play a game. "Just because you're a super-hero doesn't mean you're automatically in charge, you know."

"I know that, Amanda," he said curtly, choosing not to look at her with that particular scowl plastered across his lips. "I just... you shouldn't have to see this."

The smile faded from her lips, and she became serious. She reached out, touching her hand to his until both of them pressed against the door.

"Hey. It's me now," she said simply. "You don't have to be alone, because we both know you're not. And I won't have you talk to me like Julie and Cathy are the only women here that love you, okay?"

Smirking a little, Xander nodded, and the both of them opened the door together.

The walls were a plain off-white, coloured only in certain places, probably to the tastes of children that were forced to stay there long-term. They were, however, decorated with a variety of children's characters, like Mickey and Minnie, along with more masculine-definitive characters, like the Ninja Turtles and Spider-Man.

Three children were tucked into their beds. One was a young girl no more than seven, her hair vanished from chemo treatments and her head covered in lumps and scars. A boy looked to be asleep, but his eyes were open, a machine beside him helping him breathe. Another boy seemed to be sleeping peacefully at a weird angle to accommodate his various I.V.'s.

Mandy sighed, looking away from the little girl suffering from cancer.

"No child should have to go through this," she said, curling her lips in disgust.

Xander, still dripping Womb-blood but not caring, rushed to Mandy's side. He propped her head up on his lap and he brushed the hair out of her broken face.

She tried to speak to him, but he shook his head.

"Shh..." he cautioned, hot tears streaming down his face as he held her close, her body... so cold. "Don't speak. It's gonna be okay. You're gonna be okay, I'm gonna get you help, love. Don't you -"

She raised a hand up to the side of his face and stroked it softly.

The last of the Womb's flesh dripped off him.

"So," she whispered hoarsely. "You're the guy everybody's been talking about..."

Her hand fell from his face to the ground with an unceremonious thud, leaving only the blood that had been on her hand behind. Several long moments passed, as Xander listened to her heart slow... then finally come to a stop.

His lower lip quivered as he reached up and closed her eyes for her, those beautiful, sparkling eyes that now seemed so dull and faded. Tears pitted against her cheeks, but she made no move to wipe them off. Slowly, he wrapped his arms around her and began rocking back and forth, cradling Mandy as the tears rushed from his eyes and nose.

"You're right," Xander said, shaking off the thought. "No child should."

"I don't understand. Why are we even down here? You can fight lots of things, Xander, but death isn't one of them."

"I know that," he said bluntly, never once turning to look at her. "Believe me, Mandy, more than you'll ever realize, I know that. But these kids didn't die. They were killed."

Mandy stopped walking, allowing him to get a pace or two ahead of her, before finally having to ask. "Kids? As in, plural?"

"Yeah," Xander whispered, touching the cold sheets of an empty bed. "Plural. My senses have been turned up to eleven ever since I stepped foot on this wing, and they haven't calmed down yet. Something's making them act up. Plus, that same smell that made my senses act up in the basement is here... I think at least three kids died here within the last week, not one."

"Oh..." Mandy drawled, unable to function enough to achieve a working response. "...I don't know what to say to that."

"I know," he said, finally glancing back at her from over his shoulder. "That's what makes you human."

"Who are you talking too?" Came a small voice from one of the corner beds.

Xander turned, noticing the child for the first time. He quickly turned back to Mandy but couldn't find her. He stared at where she had been for a moment before turning back to the child.

She was a beautiful young girl, no more than ten years old. Her hair was a very light brunette, probably just now turning from the blonde it must have been all though her early childhood. She was healthily plump. Her eyes were a deep sea green, like someone else he'd known not too long ago.

"Nobody," he said, realizing that he had yet to responded.

She shrugged, then turned back to her colouring book

full of images of children playing safely. There was one image of a boy playing in the street, with a car coming toward him. The girl finished colouring the boy's hair blonde (inside the lines for the most part), then turned the page to reveal the same boy with one foot in a cast sitting in a hospital bed. Again, she began to colour, this time starting with the blonde hair, as she already had that colour out.

Xander walked over to her, careful to keep a respectful distance from her. "What are you doing there?" he asked, trying to sound as nice as he could.

"Colouring. Duh," she said under her breath, as she picked up a cornflower blue crayon.

Xander laughed at himself a little. "Yeah. I guess that was a pretty silly question, huh?"

She did not respond, merely finished with the blue and picked up an orchid purple and started to scrawl away at the page.

"Man, you are really bad with kids," Mandy laughed, peeking over the girl's shoulder.

He ignored her, trying to think of something to say to the child.

"If you want her to pay attention to you, you're going to have to stop treating and thinking of her like a child, for starters," she said, righting herself and walking around the bed, strolling past him to look at some of the books on a shelf in the corner. "Ask the kid her name, at least."

Xander coughed, telling himself that he would have thought of that eventually. "Hey, I'm Xander. What's your name?"

"Chanelle Patricia McDonald," she said, not looking

at him at first, then turning toward him with her nose scrunched up. "You have a really weird name."

"Yeah," Xander smiled. "It is kinda weird, isn't it? My real name is Alexander."

"Then why do people call you that?" She asked, turning back to her colouring book and grabbing a dark red from her crayon box.

He smirked, looking down for a moment. Across the room, Mandy turned to listen as well. "Well, when I was born my Mom died, and I don't know what happened to my Dad, so, I was given to some very nice ladies for them to take care of. They named all the little babies that they found after saints. I was named after Saint Alexander, but I was the third one, so instead of Alexander or Alex, they called me Xander."

The little girl looked up, and just as Mandy smiled at Xander so did she. "Did you get new parents?"

"Oh, yes," Xander said, sitting down on the corner of the child's bed. "I got new parents, and they loved me very much. And I have lots of friends, and I'm very happy now. And, at least I wasn't like the kid who must have come after me, because if I had been him I might have been called Lex, and that just would have had too many implications."

"What do you mean?"

"Nothing," he laughed, mostly to himself, but he heard Mandy giggle out of the corner of his ear.

There was a silence then, as the child continued to scribble away on her book.

"Can I... see what you're working on there?" Xander asked, rising up a little, trying to catch a peek.

"No!" The child protested, shielding to picture with her body, glaring at him.

Xander stepped back a little, retracting the hand he had extended toward the child's activity book. "Okay. That's... that's okay," he said soothingly, crumpling his forehead. He glanced down at the girl's arms, seeing that they were bruised and swollen, her legs larger than normal as well. He sighed, then got up to walk away.

-Plip-

Chanelle laid the book down on the bed for him to see.

Xander's eyes went wide. His hand trembled as he picked up the book.

What had originally been a boy in a hospital bed with one leg in a cast and a doctor coming in through the near-by door had been turned into the same boy with dark red smears dripping from his eyes, mouth and ears. The doctor had been coloured in black, making him look shadowy and evil.

Xander coughed slightly, as Mandy came over next to him, shaking her head at the image.

"Chanelle, where did you get the idea for this?" He asked, trying not to sound as alarmed as he actually was.

"It's what happened to the others. Matthew, Darryl, and Justin. It came and it got them. And it killed them. Nobody else can see it, but we can. And it's going to kill me to. It's going to come and kill me tonight."

"Oh, really?" Mandy said, forcing a smile.

"And what makes you think that?" Xander added, trying not to sound mean.

"Because he told me so," Chanelle said, meeting Xan-

Inner Child

der's stare with cold, hard desperation.

Xander just watched her for a minute as she turned to the next page in her book, featuring a little girl playing in her sandbox.

He turned, shot a glance at Mandy, then marched back out the door the way he'd come.

This time he made no effort to unclench his fists.

Mandy followed close behind him, trying to keep up.

CHAPTER ELEVEN
KNOWLEDGE

Mike opened the door to Coral Beach High and let Cathy in, then followed behind her. The hinge stuck for a moment, frozen at the half-closed mark, then slammed shut with a bang that echoed through the school.

The halls were empty, and carried the sounds of their footfalls all the way down the corridor. All of the students were gone now, and if the cars in the parking lot were any indication most of the staff was too. Principal Schneider was still there; he stayed late most days. Carter was still there, too. The building wouldn't be closed and locked completely for another few hours, whenever Mr. Larkin was done his cleaning rounds.

"Now that we're here, I'm not sure I totally get this," Cathy said. She was holding out her right hand as she walked and letting it brush along the combination locks on every locker they passed, the rattle it made echoing off the tiles and coming right back at her. "We're going to the library to look up people-killing monsters?"

"In this town you'd have to narrow your search a little

more than that," Mike mumbled. He was looking in each classroom they passed as they walked by, and he paused briefly when he found one that actually had someone still inside it. Mrs. Carter was sitting at her desk correcting history papers. He looked at her for a moment, then moved on past. "But no, I don't think that will get us anywhere."

"What are we going to do then? Do we have a plan other than look stuff up?"

He opened the doors to the library, again letting her step in first before following her. "*Coral Beach Daily* is a small time newspaper with an idiot for an editor and an even worse tech staff. Their website is just purple font on a white background that tells people how to subscribe to the paper."

"And?"

"And if we were in any town *but* Coral Beach, we could do what I wanted to do online... but since we're in terminally-stuck-in-the-eighties-ville, we've got to do this the low-tech way."

He made his way to a long row of desks against the back wall that were covered in heavy blue tablecloths. He pulled up one cloth, saw there was nothing underneath, and dropped it.

"Still not sure I get it."

"Miles has a deal with the editor over at the *Daily*. Every year they get a big, hard-copy edition of all their issues printed for reference." He pulled up the next cloth and revealed a long row of tall bound books. "Last decade or so, they've gotten *two* printed."

She smiled at him as he reached down and withdrew three of the large books in one armload, slamming them down on a nearby desk. "I'm impressed. I had no idea you had knowledge."

"I don't have it. I just know where it's kept," he smirked.

They looked at each other for a moment, and became very aware of the fact that they were alone.

He coughed. "I was thinking that maybe we could go back and see just how many kids have died in that children's ward or at that hospital, and going back how far. I mean, if this thing is real, it didn't just appear, right? It must have been doing this for a while, either here or at towns close to here."

"Right..." Cathy nodded, grabbing one of the volumes. "I'll check the records for Coral Cove too. But like you said, around here you can't throw a stone without hitting a mysterious death."

"Only for the past year or so," Mike reminded her, taking back the volume she'd gotten and replacing it with an older one. "So disregard all information after that point as being biased, and concentrate on things before it."

She nodded, then opened the book as he disappeared below the table again, coming back with more volumes. Each book had roughly six months worth of papers in them, each paper ten pages long. She quickly started figuring out how many pages she had to skip in order to quickly reach the headline and obituary section of each issue.

"Can we talk about it yet?" She asked after a few minutes, turning the page and not looking at him.

He paused, and then laid the books down beside her with a hard thud.

"No," he said simply, then turned back to the shelves.

"How long do you think it'll be?"

"It was my fault, Cat. Xander trusted me to find her, and I couldn't. I should have followed my instincts. I didn't. So, you know what, it might be a while."

"It wasn't your fault. It wasn't anyone's fault except for Warren and Randy and the Tees," she yelled through clenched teeth, managing to make it into a whisper.

"I know that," he said, tapping his head. "Up here, I do know that. But there's no telling it to my heart."

She sighed, nodding in defeat as she realized that the conversation was over. She had already gotten more out of him than he had initially wanted to give.

He laid down three more volumes, then stopped and stared at the bookshelf along the adjacent wall.

It took her a moment to realize that he'd stopped, and when she did she looked up and watched him. "What's wrong?"

His mouth was dry as he stepped forward and ran his hand across a row of old books. They were arid and musty and smelled the way wood left out in the rain to rot smelled. Each one was a different colour, with their titles usually printed in tiny black ink at the top of the spine and then taped on again by the librarian at the bottom in much larger print.

She looked up and found that he was in the Classics section.

He ran his finger over *Alice in Wonderland, Beauty and the Beast,* and *Jekyll and Hyde* before finally coming to a rest of *Grimm's Fairy Tales.*

He turned and headed toward the door without a word.

"Where are you going?" She asked, flopping her hands onto the desk.

"I just realized."

"Realized what?"

"I *do* have knowledge," he said cryptically, leaving the room and letting the door close silently behind him.

Cheryl Carter ran her fingers through her curly gray hair, glaring down at the pile of papers before her, only half of which were done. She circled an "it's," used where there should have been an "its," mentally cursing the Language Arts teacher down the hall for not drilling proper grammar into the students' heads more thoroughly. Her eyes had grown red from staring at the tiny type (for which she had began to mark down for, as she had specifically requested twelve point double-spaced) and her trademark smile had slowly withered into a frown.

"Dammit," she said under her breath, clenching one of the papers until it began to wrinkle.

"Bad time?" Mike said from the doorway, making her jump.

She turned swiftly to see who it was, then smiled as she recognized him, her eyes automatically softening. "Not at all," she said warmly, motioning for the seat next to her desk. "Although I wonder what brings you here this late in the afternoon."

"Research," he answered half-truthfully, sitting down. "Actually, I was wondering if you could help me out with that."

"Not a problem," she smiled, pushing the papers away symbolically. "Anything to get me away from these. Nobody is passing this paper. I'm getting more and more annoyed with every single one. I am not kidding."

"Really? I did so good in History last year."

"Yes, well, maybe that's because you never said that America was founded by Christopher Christ."

"That might have had something to do with it, yes."

"Yes. Anyway, what can I help you with?" She said, resisting the urge to go on about the papers.

"Well, do you remember that chapter we did on urban legends? I'm doing a paper on one of them, I was wondering if you could help me out."

"No problem. Which one in particular?"

Mike smiled, laughing at himself even as he said the words. "The Boogey Man."

CHAPTER TWELVE
SWING SHIFT

Xander sat in the uncomfortable chair outside Julie's hospital room again, this time leaning back no matter what he feared it was doing to his spine. He had a newspaper opened in from of him, and was currently perusing the local section.

"I'd like to know what you're doing," Mandy said, leaning in between him and the paper to try and get his attention. And failing. "No wonder I thought Mike was the one with powers for so long. At least he does something."

He continued to sit, turning to page A5 to read about the staff changes at the Mayer, Summers, and Soul law firm.

"Seriously. Do something."

"I prefer to delegate," he replied dryly, scanning down over the page. "Work smart, not hard."

"That is bullshit!" She yelled, then turned to make sure she hadn't attracted the attention of the big-breasted nurse at her station. The nurse did not react at all, as if Mandy had never spoken. "That's bullshit," she said again, in a much lower tone.

Xander peeked over the tip of the paper at the nurse as well, then up at the clock on the wall. He watched it for a moment to make sure the second hand was still ticking away correctly, checked the time on his own watch, and then went back to his paper.

"Hey, crazy guy? That's my sister in there. You'd better get on saving her."

"It's not your sister, it's your cousin."

"She's *like* a sister."

"You fight constantly."

"That is how she's like a sister."

Xander frowned, then shrugged. He couldn't fault her logic.

The minute hand on the clock switched to the fifty-nine mark.

Mandy stared at him in stunned silence, then slapped her hands to her knees and stood up. She paced all the way to the wall, then turned around and pointed at him. "You talk and you talk about taking action... about *becoming* something you can stand to look at, but look at you! You're just sitting there! There is something in this hospital killing kids, and you're just sitting there! What the fuck is wrong with you?"

Xander reached into his breast pocket and pulled out his pack of cigarettes. There was one left, which he removed and placed behind his ear. He kept the pack in his hand.

"And now you're going to go have another smoke. That's just great. Because that worked *so well* the last time.

You know what you are? I don't even know what you are. If I could come up with a word for what you are, it would be nasty. It would be like some kind of weird combination of cunt and bastard all rolled up into one and - -"

The minute hand on the clock switched over to zero.

The fat nurse got up and grabbed her lunch bag.

Xander stood up and let his paper fall to the chair behind him.

"Where are you going now?" Mandy demanded as he walked away. When he didn't stop she went after him. "I wasn't done."

"It's six o'clock," he said, not even really watching as the nurse turned around the corner to the elevators and out of sight. "Swing shift."

"Swing shift? What's that supposed to mean?"

He sat down in the nurse's chair and dumped the contents of his cigarette pack out. Flakes of nicotine sprinkled down onto the desk, followed by a small hunk of plastic and metal.

It was a thumb drive.

He plugged it in to the USB slot on the front of the nurse's computer tower, and watched as the logon screen on the monitor flashed away.

"What're you doing?" Mandy hissed, ducking down below the desk even though there was no one around.

"The day nurse has OCD," he replied softly as he opened the charts for the pediatric ward.

"And?"

"And she'd leave at six o'clock even if there was nobody there to relieve her. She'd leave at six o'clock if she were in the middle of trying to resuscitate a dead baby.

She'd leave at six even if it meant she would fall down dead."

"And what makes you so sure the swing shift nurse is going to be late?"

He allowed himself a little smile. "I have it on good authority that her car has been impounded."

Mandy stared at him for a long moment. "You're evil."

"You have no idea," he said, moving deeper into the sub files. "I'm locked out of some."

"What does that mean?"

"It means I'm locked out of some," he frowned, moving quickly from one file to the next. "All of them living patients though. All of them under the care of a..." He made several loud clacks on the keyboard. "... Dennis Marx."

"I know him."

He turned to check the physical register next to him. "He's one of four peds supervisors here. Bit of a specialist. Did his internship at the Mayo Clinic and spent three years in Doctors Without Borders..."

"You're getting all that from the chart?"

"No, I'm down in records now. Trying to find a way around those folders locks."

Her eyebrows shot up, and she turned toward the screen.

"He was kicked out. For some kind of malpractice."

"That explains how he ended up at Coral Beach."

"I think it got overturned, but it's still in here... and most of the kids that have died in the ward in the past year have been under his care. A good chunk of them while he was on duty."

He got up and unplugged the drive from the front of the computer, which promptly returned to its logon screen. He took a look around, then stepped out from around the divider and back down the hall toward his seat.

"What about the locked files?" Mandy asked, hopping to catch up to him.

He patted his pants pocket.

"You copied them to the drive?"

"I copied *everything* to the drive," he drawled, sitting down and spreading his paper out in front of him again.

Mandy stared at him dumbfounded, then smiled.

ʎʎ

Dr. Marx stepped into private room 1033 with his lab coat pulled tight around his waist. The light above the door shone down on his bald head and the few hairs that clung to it and made it look like a halo, but even that couldn't make him look angelic... the extra light just made the rest of his head look hollowed out and dark.

Billy Reynolds clutched the sheets on either side of his bed when he saw Marx, his breathing picking up speed and fogging the inside of the oxygen mask he was wearing.

Billy had gotten HIV from a blood transfusion six years ago when he was ten. Even though all the proper procedures had been apparently followed, a bag of infected blood had gotten through the federal screening process and ended up in Coral Cove, where it stayed on ice and waited for someone to need a pint of AB+. That happened less than two months later, when Billy's father had hit a deer while driving drunk with Billy in the back seat. They gave him the blood, and for four years he'd been complete-ly unaware of the time bomb coursing through his veins. He'd even lost his virginity to Karen King, something she herself has regretted ever since, even though they always wore a condom.

Then his cousin Wally had gotten sick with cancer, and Billy volunteered to give up his bone marrow. A routine blood test changed not only his life, but also the family's perceptions of which child was sick.

He only had the news three weeks when Karen broke up with him. He was on antiviral medications that made him vomit everything he put into his system for another year before the virus activated and became full-blown AIDS. Since then he'd spent more time at the hospital than he had at home. He'd lost almost a third of his body weight, his skin was a milky white, his teeth were falling out, and his lips were covered in lesions. At sixteen, Billy Reynolds was closer to death than most men of seventy. He had a lot to be scared of. Not only death, but also the process of dying... a process that would be longer and harder for him than for most.

Nothing scared him like Dr. Dennis Marx.

Marx came in and closed the door behind him, and immediately the heart monitor next to Billy picked up its pace, no longer a steady *BEEP BEEP BEEP* but a hurried, erratic *BEEP BEEBEEP BEEBEEBEEP*. He hated the heart monitor. It was next to impossible to pretend you weren't scared with that thing strapped to your arm blaring at the top of its digital lungs.

Marx let his lab coat fall open. He was carrying a met-al-and-glass syringe that was as big around as his thumb, but from Billy's point of view it was as big around as his leg.

BEEPBEEPBEEPBEEPBEEP

"Now there's no need to be frightened," Marx said, the light from the window glaring off his glasses and making them glow. He smiled that wide, funhouse smile of his as he leaned in over Billy's bed. "We're going to try and make everything all better."

Billy's eyes went wide as Marx held the needle up and flicked it twice, sending all the air to the top. He pushed the plunger and forced all the air out, the excess liquid squirting up and then back down onto his sheets. It smelled like feet.

Billy couldn't speak, couldn't move, couldn't do anything. His vision blurred as he started to cry.

Marx leaned down and inserted the needle into Billy's IV and pushed the plunger until it was empty.

The whole world went sideways as Billy's head lolled to the side, and after a moment his heart monitor slowed back to its steady *BEEP BEEP, BEEP BEEP*.

He couldn't shut his eyes but he could still see. Could still see everything as Marx leaned over him with that damned penlight and shone it in both his eyes, then ducked out of his field of vision again, revealing the air duct on the ceiling above him.

As Billy watched, horrified and unable to even say anything about it, eight long fingers made their way down from the darkness beyond the duct grate and gripped it.

Marx reached over and shut Billy's eyes.

All he could hear was the skitter scamper of thousands of little legs crawling around the metal tube.

CHAPTER THIRTEEN
BAIT

"What do you mean you haven't found anything yet?" Xander asked, leaning in as close to the payphone as he could. "It's been hours. Whatever that thing is, it could go after Julie tonight. Or Chanelle. Or both! What's taking you so long?"

"Considering that all I had to work on was: it's big and looks spooky, I think I'm doing all right," Cathy replied, trying her best to stay calm as she continued to flip through the pages, scribbling notes down into a steno book next to her as she did.

Xander sighed, pinning the phone between his ear and his shoulder. He used his free hand to wipe sweat from his brow. His other hand was busy propping him against the wall.

"Sorry," he breathed, lowering his voice as a nurse walked by. "But this place is starting to drive me around the bend. And Tommy is still in there with Julie. Seriously, doesn't that guy know the meaning of the term visiting hours?"

Cathy raised an eyebrow, shooting him a look that she hoped the silence portrayed through the phone lines.

"You have issues," she said finally.

Mike came in without a word, marching past her to the bookshelf. She turned to look at him and mouthed the word "what?"

It was ignored.

"Wait, what?" She said into the phone, grunting as she turned away from her boyfriend.

"I asked what you had so far," Xander repeated, rubbing the bridge of his nose.

"Um," Cathy replied, flipping back a page in her notebook. "There have been weird child and preteen deaths going on at this hospital and the ones in Coral Cove and other places around for almost... um, two... two decades now. But, I mean, all of the kids were sick. Most of them really sick, so I guess nobody really noticed. And there probably aren't as many as I'm seeing here, most of these probably are actually natural causes."

Mike came back from the shelf and shoved an open book in front of Cathy. Her eyes went wide. On the one page there was text, but on the adjacent page was an etched picture of a child in its bed, screaming as a creature came out of the closet at it. The monster wore overalls in this picture, along with a straw hat and a stem of wheat propped in its mouth. It had no skin, just contorted muscle tissue clinging to its bones, and it had no eyes... just a large, bulging erection in its pants as it came toward the child.

"Do you have anything else?" Xander asked, trying his best to sound patient.

"Oh, god," Cathy gasped, bringing a hand to her mouth as she read the inscription.

"What?"

"The Boogey Man, also called Fear, also called the Ok' La' Zarr... although it doesn't say in what language. It looks *exactly* like you and Julie said, Xander. Exactly. Oh." Her voice was almost a whimper.

"What?" Xander said again, paying perfect attention now. "What is it, Cat?"

"Oh, gawd, Xander. They must be so scared..."

"What? Why?"

"It... it sits on their chest and it grabs at them and cuts them and hurts them until they die, Xander. It just keeps torturing them, first mentally, then violently, until the child dies. It feeds off their fear, so it tries to keep the child alive as long as possible. Oh, gawd, Xander..."

"Okay," Xander said, clenching a fist until it bled. "Okay, it's okay. Fear... yeah, that makes sense. Is there anything else?"

"Yeah," she said, fighting back tears. "It says it's some kind of culler. That it culls the weak, traditionally. Whatever that means."

"Sick people," Mike relayed, touching her on the shoulder as he put more books in front of her.

"Sick people," she repeated into the phone, her hand rising to meet with his.

"Makes sense, as much as any of this does," Xander sighed, turning to see Tommy walking down the hall toward him.

"I don't know if it's part of what it needs or if it's just because sick kids are scared or what, but... oh, you've got to find this thing, Xander. You've got to stop it."

"I gotta go. Tommy's here."

"But what are you going to..."

"I'll handle it," he snapped, hanging up the phone and turning to Tommy.

"Hey, man," Tommy smiled, nodding politely.

"Hey," Xander reciprocated. "How is she?"

"Tired now. A nurse came in and gave her some pain-killers. She sad that they'd knock her out, so I got scarce."

Xander nodded.

"You didn't have to stick around, y'know."

Xander smiled. "I got other people here."

"We all do," Tommy groaned. "Where's everyone else?"

"Home. Where I'm going," he said as a way of terminating the conversation, turning and walking away. "You should too, man. This place'll kill you after a while."

"Yeah," Tommy agreed, turning toward the exit. "I know exactly what you mean."

ʎ×ʎ

"Hello?" Cathy said into the phone, tapping on the receiver a few times. "Hello? Is anybody there?"

"Is he there?" Mike asked, taking the phone away and checking it himself.

"No! Bastard!" She growled, pushing the books away from her.

"What did he say?"

"He said he'd take care of it," she yelled, running her hands through her hair. "That stubborn idiot! How's he going to fight something like that?"

Mike stopped and thought for a moment, staring down at the etching in the fairy tales book. The child in the picture looked mortified.

"By baiting it," he said simply.

He got up and motioned for her to do the same, not even taking the time to pick up his coat as he headed for the door. She followed, scooping it off the desk as she went.

ʌ>ʌ

Marx leaned over his desk, scribbling away at his calculations as the sun finished dipping below the horizon. Not that he'd noticed. He hadn't looked up from his folders since dealing with Billy Reynolds, not even to finish eating his dinner, instead leaving it to grow bad on his desk with one bite taken out of it. It was a tuna fish sandwich that his wife had made with too much mayonnaise and a healthy chunk of diced onions for some reason he couldn't fathom, so it wasn't as though he would have devoured it even under the best of circumstances.

He stared at the number eight he had just made, his lip shaking a little. The number was important somehow, he knew it. If his data was right then this wasn't the last equation by far, and yet still, it seemed very important.

"What's up, Doc?" Came a voice from beside him, where previously there had been no sound. It was thick a raspy, like a person with a cancerous throat trying to talk while chugging a glass of water. He turned, only to be hit square in the face with a powerful fist. He spun around from the force of the impact, slamming his chin against the desk before hitting the ground with an unceremonious thud.

"Always wanted to say that," Xander said through the Black Womb's mouth, his eyes glowing a bright red, reflecting the fluorescent lights back to the ceiling. His skin was black and scaly, and he nearly blended in with the deep shadows that the furniture around him cast.

He took the shopping bag off his shoulder and plopped it onto the floor, then took a look around the room. He took his thumb drive out of the bag and shoved it into the slot on the front of Marx's computer, watching as the screen hummed to life again.

"What was the point of that?" Mandy yelled, staring down at Marx. There was blood coming out of a gash on his head. "He could be hurt."

"He could also be a Mormon," Xander snarled, double-clicking on the three encrypted files he'd transferred to the drive and then stepping out from around the desk. "I couldn't really give a shit about either fact right now."

"The files? Is that what all this was about?" She asked, leaning in and watching as the progress bar sped across the screen. "Couldn't you have just broken in at home?"

"Could have. Didn't want to. Several reasons," he said, but did not elaborate as to what those reasons were. His long tongue made him lisp on the *ess* sound at the beginning of several, but she didn't call him on it.

She watched as he scanned the room with those big red eyes of his, then finally found the fridge and walked toward it.

"What's in there?"

"What we came here for," he said, picking up the lock.

"You got some sort of fancy spy-thing for picking that

too?"

"Yep," he said, pulling down on the lock hard and snapping it off.

Mandy's eyes widened.

He opened the refrigerator door and saw the long case of vials on top. He grabbed it by both sides and let it fall to the floor, all the vials shaking violently in their holsters.

"Watch it," Mandy said, jumping a little.

He pulled one of the vials out and looked at the label. It said anthrax. He put it to one side.

"Anthrax? What's he doing with anthrax?"

"No idea," he growled, shooting a look at Marx's unconscious form.

"Wait, what are you doing with anthrax?"

"Thing feeds on fear," he said, even as he picked up another vial marked Ebola and laid it down with the first. "That's why it's been hanging out in hospitals the last twenty years or so. Kids are easy to make afraid, even easier when they're sick. Even easier for parents to pass it off when you can write it off as fever dreams."

"And?"

"And now it's in Coral Beach... and thanks to me, this whole town is jumping scared. Fucking thing has an all-you-can-eat buffet." He picked up a vial of red liquid marked REYNOLDS - HIV, stared at it a moment, then put it back down.

"I'm following you. I am. *Why do you have Ebola and anthrax?*"

He took out a third vial and laid it with the other two, then grabbed all three and got to his feet.

"*And* influenza?"

"When the thing came at me the first time I was scared... scared about what was going to happen with me and Julie, more scared than I think I've ever been."

"Okay."

He frowned. "Not scared now. I like having something to hit, something to fight."

He sighed, then popped the tops off of all three of the vials and grabbed the half-filled coffee mug off of Marx's desk.

He turned to Mandy, who looked at him in horror.

"Gotta get scared," he whispered, pouring all three into the mug. He watched as the liquids seemed to disappear amidst the black caffeine.

"Here's to my health," he said sarcastically, shooting the liquid down his throat as fast as possible, then throwing the cup against the far wall and smashing it to pieces.

Mandy cringed, backing away from him a pace and almost tripping over the remaining vials.

He stood there for a moment, wondering if the drink would do anything to him, or if his healing factor would dispose of the toxins before they made their way into his system. He got his answer suddenly as he bent over, pain erupting from his gut as if it were on fire. The room started to spin in three directions at once, making him want to vomit. Blood started to dribble out of his mouth, and his hands and feet felt like jelly. It seemed impossible for him to stand or even crawl toward the door.

"Come on," he said angrily, clenching his jagged teeth as he stared at the open doorway in front of him, just a few feet away a moment ago, now miles and miles distant. "Come on, Drew."

The blackness ebbed off his body, losing its consistency until it was like dark water, pouring off onto the floor around him, revealing Xander. He was naked and covered in a thin layer of congealed blood. Slowly, every second aching, he reached for the bag he had dropped next to the desk and took his shoes out, along with his socks, shirt, and pants.

Every motion killing him, feeling like swords made out of fire were slashing through him, he pulled on his clothes and took his thumb drive out of the computer, then started his way down the hall, hugging the wall to try to keep himself from falling over and passing out.

"Black... Womb lives," he said half-jokingly, letting the smile fade quickly as it hurt his face to wear it. He made his way down toward the children's ward.

"This was a really bad idea," Mandy stated, walking along next to him with her hands clasped firmly behind her back.

"Than... ku. F'input," Xander said, shooting her a look. The words had made perfect sense to him, but took a second for her to translate.

"You're welcome," she frowned. "Stutter much? It was probably that anthrax... or maybe it was the Ebola?"

"Didn saw u comin up wit anie bright deias," he mumbled, stumbling and banging his knee against the wall. He grunted, then continued staggering forward, only pulling it together enough to stand when a nurse passed by him.

"You know, I think there was a strand or two of the AIDS virus in that fridge back there. Maybe you should take that with some Jack Daniels, just for good measure."

"Ew could help, y'know."

"I could... but this was your brilliant plan. Kill yourself and save this thing the trouble. A time saver, granted, but otherwise not your best work."

He paused, his eyes growing distant. "Ben making a lot of bad mistakes eight Lee."

"Yea. Well, no argument here," she groaned. "Trying to kill yourself is one thing, now you wanna make yourself suffer, too? You're going for the gold."

"No more children will die because of this thing, or because I failed to act," he said, turning angrily toward her. But again, she wasn't there. Sighing, he turned and continued staggering down the hall toward the children's ward.

Mike and Cathy ran down the street that they had come up just a few hours ago, their chests aching for them to stop, for them to let their lungs rest.

"I don't understand," Cathy gasped, stopping for a moment. She rested her hands against her kneecaps, took a deep breath, then started again. "What's he going to do? How's he going to fight it?"

"He's going to make himself scared," Mike replied grimly, still moving forward in the direction of the hospital. "He's going to negate the Womb and make himself scared. He's going to fight that thing without his powers, and sick to boot."

Cathy wrinkled her brow at him. "But he'd be as helpless as one of those children. That'd be suicide!"

"Exactly," Mike said, his voice deep and dark.

Cathy's eyes grew wide.

Chanelle McDonald pulled the covers high around her head, not letting any light into her private little cave she had created for herself.

She shivered, even though it was very warm in the room and even warmer curled up the way she was. She whined a bit, no matter how much she tried to stop herself from doing so. Fresh tears joined the old ones as they tumbled down her cheeks, making sudden plopping noises as they fell onto the paper sheets.

The room got colder all of a sudden, although it was still very warm. It was a different sort of cold. A frost that did not attack the skin or the muscles, instead bypassing all of this and chilling you in your bones, making them ache in pain with the cold.

There was a slithering sound, moving quickly from one part of the room to another, scattered all about, as if even the noise itself wasn't quite sure where it was coming from.

Another child, one of the boys, started to cry.

The slithering went close to him for a moment, then started frolicking about the room again... like a child in a candy store, unable to chose which treat it wanted first.

There was an odor, a sickly sweet stench like sugar water and vomit. It filled the air all around her, attacking from all sides and forcing itself into her nostrils until it was all she could smell, all she could taste.

She felt something run over her, like light fingers over her sheets.

Suddenly, something ripped the blankets off her, as quick as a flash. She turned to face it and started to scream, but it shoved its hand over her throat before she had a chance, muffling the sound of her voice. Its hand felt too soft... slimy and sticky. It was only when it came into the light that Chanelle realized that it had no flesh, just muscles and strips of twine holding them to the bone.

"Shh," the creature soothed, as the sweet smell turned into a taste, one that dripped off its hands in long globs and traveled down her throat. "Nothing to fear..." it said, revealing a mouth full of gums, no teeth to speak of, just rotting, decayed gums that smelled like a dead skunk. Its other hand was grabbing at its own crotch, feeling itself through the folds of its pressed suit, grunting ever so slightly as it did so, sending bursts of rot and bile onto Chanelle's face with each sound.

"Nothing to fear..." it said again, almost musical in its tone. It smiled, although without skin it was hard to tell it from the twitching muscles of its face.

It opened its eyes at her, revealing them to be nothing but gaping black holes, voids of nothing that seemed to go on forever...

... like the abyss.

She tried to scream again, but the sound was still muffled by the demon's hand, and she only got herself a mouthful of the goo that covered his body for her trouble.

"...Nothing to fear..." it repeated again, chanting it now as if it were a mantra, calm in its voice even as he struggled with the child. The fear in her escalated, and the creature absorbed it all, getting every last drop that it could out of her.

It drew back and slapped her across the face, sending

her tumbling to the floor, splattering a trail of its slime across the wall. She tried to get up and run, but it was on her much too fast, grabbing her by her tiny hips and slamming her against her bedside table, again knocking her to the floor.

"Help!" She screamed as loud as she could, making it remember to cover her mouth. She tried again, but it muffled her voice.

It smiled broadly with its toothless, skinless mouth as it unbuttoned its pants and began to pull them down.

"Nothing to fear... but fear itself." It almost giggled, revealing itself not to have a penis or anything resembling one, but rather two great red eyes that stared at her, burning with eternal flame, hungering for more of her. One last time, she tried to scream.

"Hey," came a weak voice from the doorway, drawing both the girl and the creature's attention. There, slumped against the doorway just to keep himself from falling face first to the ground, mucus and blood running from his nose, his guts on fire... was Xander.

"Keep it in your pants," he glowered, staggering toward the villain.

The demon hissed, grabbing Chanelle by the arm and rising to its feet, holding her out. She dangled about a foot from the floor, tears streaming down her face.

It looked from Xander to Chanelle, then back again. Something deep inside those hollowed out eyes sparkled.

"Yeah, I'm a much nummier treat, aren't I?" He smiled, coughing up a great mound of blood. "Why don't you give up the girl and come on over to man land? I'll give you a nice treat of big dirty fear."

It squirmed its toes, and that scuttling sound of thousands of legs filled the room again. It was happy, Xander realized.

He squinted, both out of confusion and because from his point of view there were three demons and three girls, and he wasn't sure if he could fight all of them at once.

It crouched and dug the sharp edges of its fingers into the bruised fat of Chanelle's arm.

"Ooh, scary," Xander said, wobbling a little, waving his fingers in front of his face for effect. "Hey, you wanna know what's even scarier than that?" he poised, stopping shy of the tall, skinny creature, looking up at it so that they were almost nose-to-nose.

The creature opened its mouth, a long string of clicks coming out of it, as it tilted its head to the side, as if to ask: *What?*

"Me."

He drew back hard, aiming to hit the creature square between the eyes, instead landing the punch on its left shoulder, causing it to drop the girl onto the floor, allowing her to get away. She screamed loudly, and the other three children got out of bed and ran out while she hid underneath her bed, leaving Xander alone with it.

The creature righted its posture, staring down at Xander with big, blank eyes, its mouth open in a joker-like sadistic smile.

"You... *are* afraid," it drawled, in a voice that reminded Xander of a cartoon snake with a throat infection.

"Of ewe?" Xander smirked, almost falling over all on his own, his eyes glazing over as sweat began to bead and dribble down across his face, tasting salty when it reached his lips in large quantities. "I was. But now... Why would eye bee scared of ewe?"

The demon backhanded Xander across the chin fast, sending him flying across the room. He landed on one of the children's beds, breaking the springs in the mattress before rolling off onto the floor and hitting his head.

"I see," he grumbled to himself, even as the creature walked toward him, the slithering sound coming from everywhere. He tried to get up and face the thing again, but was instead forced back onto his knees by the burning in his stomach. He clutched his sides and threw up, splattering warm bile all over the floor.

"Guh," he gasped, breathing deep, wiping the puke and snot away from the lower half of his face.

"Brilliant," he said sardonically, cursing himself. "Five minutes into the fight and I've managed to heave all over myself. This is fifth grade all over again."

The creature grabbed him by the scruff of his shirt and flung him across the room. He smashed into the far wall, removing paint and plaster with the impact. It sprinkled down upon him as he lay dead-to-the-world on the floor, drool coming out of the left side of his mouth, blood out of the right.

"You fear life," the creature stated, suddenly next to Xander again, lifting him up by his collar.

Xander fumbled around a nearby desk, trying to grab at something that he could use for a weapon, finding nothing. He gasped for air, and the bits that he did get were further stifled by his stuffed nose and sinuses. The world waved about before him, shaking and convulsing with each hit he took as the creature held him up with one arm and slapped his head back and forth with the other, laughing mechanically as it did so.

"You fear living," it reiterated, slapping Xander again.

"You prey on the sick, the people that can't defend themselves," Xander spat, fighting for the breath and strength to form each word. "That tells me something too: you're afraid of losing. You're afraid to fight fair. Oh, scary. A monster only fit to hunt scared, sick children. I cower. I may be scared of a lot of things..." he said, glaring at where the demons eyes would be. "But you're not one of them."

He reached out fast, grabbing at its tender facial muscles and digging his nails in, ripping off its face, expecting to find a mass of bone. Instead there was nothing, just the same abyss that made up its eyes. The creature screamed, clutching at the void that Xander had created.

Its hand disappeared into its face.

Then its arm.

Slowly, its entire body was sucked into its own face, imploding upon itself as the hissing, slithering sound became deafening, and its scream seemed to pierce the very walls of reality. Xander watched in horror and shock, as the creature finally blipped out of existence.

Mike burst in through the door, sending it slamming against the wall.

"Xander!" He screamed, seeing his friend standing there, looking dazed and confused. He looked around the room helplessly, panic washing over him as Cathy came in behind him. "Xander, I can't see it! Tell em where it is so I can help!"

Xander smiled, raising an arm to point and laugh at his friend, when in fact he was pointing just a little to the left. The effort made the blood rush to his head, and his eyes rolled back as he fell to the floor, hitting his head off the footboard of the bed as he did.

Mike and Cathy both looked at him, their eyebrows raised.

CHAPTER FOURTEEN
ONE WEEK LATER

Xander lay in his bed, smiling, as the fan his Mother had brought up from downstairs for him turned toward him again, blowing his hair back. He laughed to himself, taking another gaping handful of salt-and-vinegar chips and shoving as many of them in his mouth as would fit, then tried hard to chew, still grinning like an idiot.

"Hey!" Cathy groaned in a cute, flu voice, her lower lip protruding. "Stop hogging all the chips."

"My chips," Xander said territorially, hugging them closer and sniffing back mucus. "Not your chips. My chips."

"It speaks," Mike said, then sneezed, wiped his nose with a well-used tissue, then turned back to them. "First time in twenty minutes."

"Hey!" Xander said, pointing at the computer he had hooked up to play movies for the three of them. "I've been watching the - -" he paused, looking at the blank screen.

"You stared at the credits rolling for ten minutes, the blank screen for five, and then you became very interested in the fan until a moment ago," Cathy informed him. "Looking after you is like watching one of those Discovery Channel specials on autism, I swear."

"Quiet."

She rolled her eyes and sniffed back a helping of phlegm. "I think the anthrax would have done it, you know. You could have kept it confined to the non-contagious illnesses."

"I couldn't take chances," he shrugged, an act that caused his shoulders to ache violently.

"Did you ever get those files cracked after?" Mike asked, motioning toward the thumb drive that rested atop Xander's keyboard.

"Ayuh."

"And?"

"And Dennis Marx was a douche-bag... just not a child-killing douche-bag."

"Then what was - -"

"Was trying to come up with a cure for a couple of different diseases. Found this weird kind of kola plant while he was in Niger that he was convinced had medicinal properties... tried testing it on a bunch of locals without their consent, got him drummed out of Doctors Without Borders... but he never *killed* anyone. Far as I can tell, not even his treatments harmed anyone. May have not made them better, but didn't harm."

"But, why would that thing have been so interested in his patients?"

"Like I said: guy was a douche-bag. Had no bedside manner. To me and you, that's just annoying... To a sick kid, it's terrifying."

Mike sighed, laying his back down against the pillow.

Cathy frowned, then held out her hand to Xander.

"Give chips," she ordered.

"Not your chips," he repeated. "*My* chips."

"Give her the frigging chips," Mandy moaned from her seat at Xander's desk, wearing a flannel nightie that was just a little too small for her. "The only thing worse than having to be sick is having to listen to you two bitch while being sick."

Xander groaned, then tossed the bag of chips onto Cathy's lap. She gave a handful to Mike immediately, who thanked her with a kiss.

Mandy looked at the two of them, resting her chin on her wrist and smiling. "Those two'll never stop, will they?" She remarked to Xander, as both Mike and Cathy watched each other's movements longingly.

"No, they won't," he replied groggily.

"What?" Mike asked, smiling.

"You two. You two will never stop loving each other. Even when you guys went through that rough spot, there was still so much love there. It was like, you couldn't be that mad without passion, and you can't have that kind of passion without love... y'know?"

Mike smiled, leaning in and kissing his lover.

"Yeah, I do," Cathy grinned, kissing him back. "So, what brought that out all of a sudden?"

"Ah," he said, grabbing the remote as if to disregard it. "Just thinkin' about what Mandy said."

There was silence between the three of them then, as they all avoided eye contact with each other.

"She always did know what was going on," Mike said finally, his eyes welling up although he was smiling. He grasped Cathy's hand, as tightly as he dared. "I'm really going to miss that about her. She was a special girl, wasn't she?"

"Yeah," Cathy agreed, tenderly putting pressure on his hand, stroking it with her thumb.

"A whole week of the three of you sitting there sick, and finally someone gets it out of him," Mandy tisked, flicking through the remaining movies. "Hey, how about the Ninja Turtles movie? I haven't seen that since I was a kid."

"Ninja Turtles?" Xander responded, cocking his eyebrow at her.

"All right," Mike chimed in agreement.

Cathy nodded, then got up to change the disk.

CHAPTER FIFTEEN
CH-CH-CH-CHANGES

She picked through the garbage tin that the wind had blown over a few minutes before, fumbling about it for any food that had not spoiled yet. During her years on the streets she had become adept at taking advantage of the wastefulness of humans, a trait to which they seemed to ascribe in endless amounts.

With her keen vision she found a small scrap of ham still moist with sauce sticking out from underneath a battered can of preserved beans. She reached out slowly and carefully, always mindful of her surroundings, then finally hooked it and pulled it out from beneath the can. It fell to the ground in front of her. She brought it to her mouth immediately, clutching it between her teeth and feeling the rich, flavorful texture against her tongue.

The porch light came on.

She turned and ran into the woods without so much as looking where she was going, so fast that Ms. Engleman did not even see the blur of motion she created as she zipped away. She still clutched the chunk of meat between her teeth, so tightly that she was afraid she would bite through it and send the excess falling into the grass below her.

When the light was obscured by a large oak tree she stopped, still able to hear Ms. Engleman shuffling about on her front step but knowing well that she was safe. She laid the meat down on the ground and, holding it down with her paws, began to tear away at it with her sharp teeth.

Her name had been Tawny once, and she was a tabby cat. At least she had been, before her owners had moved and not taken her with them. Now, she was just a stray. She closed her eyes and started to purr happily as the sugary taste of marinated pork bathed her taste buds and found its way down her throat.

The oak next to her made a long, croaking sound as it settled. It sounded like a frog at rest on a lily pad.

She stopped eating, her ears going flat against her head as she glared out into the open wood. There was nothing around her, just the black silhouettes of trees painted on the blue curtain of the night.

Tentatively, she turned back toward her feast.

Suddenly she found herself hoisted into the air, the skin on her neck and face pulling tight and making it nearly impossible to move. She hissed, flailing and spinning and trying to make contact at her assailant with her claws.

Her eyes went wide as she felt something penetrate her gullet, going in fast and coming out the other side. Her growl slowly faded until there was nothing, and she went limp.

\(^\)

"Stop it..." she giggled, gently moving his hands away from her hips, but making no effort to stop him as he put them there again. She laughed as he groped at her loose clothing, pulling it and then stopping, biting his lip with temptation.

"Why should I?" He cooed, looking around and seeing nothing but the back porch of her house between the trees just beyond her yard. "Nobody can see us..."

Trina Kennessy smiled as John brushed his hand along the side of her face, the tips of his fingers gingerly tickling the short hairs on the back of her neck as he did, sending cold shivers up and down her spine. "Cathy walks back this way sometimes. What if she..."

"She won't," John whispered in a hushed voice, grabbing her by the waist to bring her up close enough to give him a kiss. He was much taller than her, and quite a bit older as well. She melted into the kiss, barely noticing as his hands inched their way up the inside of her shirt and began to fondle her breasts. She bit her lip, stark white on top of lush red. She ran her hands through his gelled blonde hair, the pointed tips pricking at her as she did. She started to pull away just a little, but he kissed her deeper, bringing her back into the moment.

Her hair was a dark black much like her sister's, and was pulled back in a pony tail until she reached up and let go, allowing it to fall to the moss covered ground next to the tree roots below. She finally realized that he was touching her, and she smiled, reaching around to the back of her shirt. She fumbled for just a second then took her bra out through her left sleeve.

He smiled hungrily, his thumbs touching her nipples underneath the shirt; he stared at the moving cloth as though he had x-ray vision. After a moment he wouldn't have needed it, as she lifted up the front of her shirt to give him a clear view of what he was doing to her. She was thin and white in the overhanging moonlight, the shadows cast by the leaves of nearby maple trees dancing over her body and making it come to life as she quivered beneath his touch.

He bent down, scooping up her tiny body and bringing it to him, his lips sucking at her breasts out of pure, uninhibited sexual starvation, making him convulse and burn for more.

"Hmm..." she giggled, laughing as she pulled the shirt back down, wrestling away from his grasp. Her hands moved quickly as he lost his grip on her, touching him ever so briefly in the place he longed for her to linger. She skipped away from him a step or two, bringing that hand up to her open, circular mouth, her tongue dancing along her own fingers, as she playfully lifted her shirt and put it back down, letting her navel appear and disappear from view.

John smiled at her, taking a step toward her.

She quickly took a step back, waving a finger in front of her, as if to say "oh-no-you-don't."

Smiling through clenched teeth, she began to play with the button of her jeans. With aching slowness she rode the top of her jeans down with her thumbs, exposing her slender midriff and the white freckled swells of her hips. He swallowed hard and took a step toward her, but she moved a step back to match, holding out a scolding finger to him and smiling.

"Catch me if you can," she laughed, turning and skipping over a log, running further into the forest.

He grinned and started after her, his mind a gaggle of things that she might let him do once he caught hold of that tiny, thin form of hers. She zigged and zagged through tree branches that scraped against the meat of her arms, but kept going, laughing and giggling all the way as evergreen needles fell into her hair. He gained on her quickly, catching her just as she was about to fall onto a log, causing them both to fall to the cold, wet ground, him on top of her.

"Oh!" He cried, feeling his own head to make sure it wasn't bleeding. "Are you okay?"

"Yeah," she said, her frown slowly returning to a smile.

His hands touched something, and her over-biting tooth again pressed against her ruby lips.

"How about now?"

"Yeah," she gasped between breaths, nodding her head quickly. "Oh, yeah." She tilted her head upward and closed her eyes as his lips started to trail down her neck, his spare hand shoving her blouse up again, revealing her small, teacup-sized breasts. She moaned, opened her eyes halfway, and then screamed.

Lying not four feet away from them was the mangled body of a German shepherd, its fur and organs spread out over a two foot radius, blood soaking the snow all around it, steam still rising from the open wounds.

Mike sat in his room and stared up at the ceiling, clenching a red stress ball in his right hand every few seconds then feeling it expand as air reentered the tiny holes on either side. He glanced at it every once and a while, its nature perplexing him, as it went from being almost flat to spherical within a matter of seconds, and then back again at his command.

"Are you having fun?" Cathy asked. She was rotating around in Mike's swirly chair, closing her eyes and then opening them again to see how each affected how fast she got dizzy.

He turned to her, watching as her spinning slowly came to a stop, until she finally put her foot down to halt it, the chair facing him, and crossed her legs.

"Actually, yes," he answered truthfully, after only a moment's hesitation to mull over whether or not this was another of her infamous trick questions that would no doubt leave him gasping for metaphorical air.

She rolled her eyes, then threw her back onto the chair, sending different parts of her hair bobbing in all directions at once, making it frizzy. She looked all around at the posters on the wall, of Curt Kobain, Megadeath and one movie poster from *The Care Bears Movie*, hidden slightly by his closet door.

"Is that Tender-Heart?" She asked, pointing at it from her relaxed pose.

He paused, sighed once, and then hung his head. "No, it's Brave-Heart Lion. That's the movie where they meet the Care Bear cousins."

"Right," she nodded, smirking as she recalled the exact plot of the movie. "Much more masculine, really. You have in no way weakened your stature as a grown heterosexual male. Not at all."

He frowned, turning to watch for shapes to appear out of his ceiling tile again, placing pressure on his ball.

"You know that only works with stucco ceilings... right?" She asked, cocking an eyebrow in his direction.

He stopped mid-squeeze, clicking his tongue against the roof of his mouth.

"Yes," he said finally. He coughed. "Have you been talking to Xander today?"

"Eh," she passed, shrugging off the notion. "He was feeling well enough to get around outside the house today, so I'm pretty sure that he's going down to the hospital to check on Julie. I don't think she's doing a whole lot better."

Mike sighed, remembering the way she had looked with bloodstained sheets wrapped around her body, trying to find a position that wouldn't send pain coursing through her. "Does he want tag-alongs? We could pick up some more candy for her, I think she should be able to eat it now."

Cathy shook her head. "No, I got the impression from Xander that, after what happened the last time, this was going to be a solo outing. I think he really wants to spend some time patching things up between them."

"Do you think he can?"

Cathy smirked. "We managed, so I guess anything's possible."

He smiled at her, getting up in one quick motion and

walking over to her, a sparkle of mischief in his eyes. He placed both of his hands on either armrest of the chair, boxing her in, in essence, then leaned in and kissed her, softly and passionately, on the lips. She tilted her head up to meet his as his tongue darted in and out of her mouth like smooth lightning. Slowly, without even realizing it, she felt her own legs uncross and move apart, spreading out before him. He paused, looking down at her lap, and his hand began to quiver. He turned his gaze back toward her, coughed again, and inched back a pace, then back again, coming in quickly to kiss her, his hands meeting with her hips and clutching them tightly.

RIIIIIING

"Aw," Mike sighed, clenching a fist playfully and softly tapping it against the arm of the chair.

"Have you... um, ever considered getting that disconnected?" Cathy asked, exhaling as though she hadn't done so in several minutes, her face red and hot.

"I was just thinking that," he drawled as he picked up the phone and brought it to his ear. "Hello?" an odd look came over his face, and then he shrugged and passed the phone to Cathy. "It's for you."

Cathy made a face, taking the phone from him. "Yeah?" she said in an almost agitated tone of voice, bringing a finger to her mouth to bite. "What?"

ʎ⋎ʎ

Jesse Larkin heaved a sigh as he stepped out of his car and into the parking lot. He always hated this time of the year, when everything was cold and wet, and the snow always came, then melted, only to come again a day or so later. He wished every time that it would simply stay for the season or leave so that spring would start, but it never did.

Soon he'd be out for winter break though, and that was always something to look forward to. But then again, after that there was midterms. And then, of course, there was the fact that soon his mother was bound to decide that it wasn't safe for him to be driving on the roads any more, just as she had last year, just weeks after he had gotten his license.

He pushed back a mound of his curly blonde hair as he locked up the car, revealing a gash near his left temple. He winced and cursed a little as his finger accidentally brushed up against it, making him grit his teeth in pain.

TUNK!

He swirled, turning to see what the noise had been, seeing nothing but the empty parking lot. He frowned to himself, then turned back and walked toward the mall. It had been closed for hours, but he still had some business to take care of out back.

There was a sound, like someone running across pavement, dragging their feet.

He turned again, this time looking all around him, examining every shadow.

"Is someone there?" He called out, his New England accent thick. "Is anyone there?"

ᚾᚷᚾ

Xander stumbled on the stairs of the hospital, catching himself before his face became a smear on the concrete steps, but not before his kneecap struck them. He grunted as he felt the pain surge up from his leg, not quite bleeding but bruised enough for blood to come to the surface anyway, making it feel moist even though it was not. He cursed on the slick walkway, then continued into the hospital, waving at a familiar nurse as he did, mentally making a note to take the wheelchair entrance for the rest of the winter. The nurse waved back to him but avoided eye contact, continuing to sort through the mounds of paperwork in front of her.

He passed by the green plastic chairs of the waiting area, its denizens each looking up at him with a mixture of envy and anger as he strolled past, bypassing the call from the receptionist and going straight through the big, white doors into the main part of the hospital.

He grinned as he passed by a wall full of pages from children's colouring books, each a different picture coloured by a different child patient. Most where incoherent scribbles by children that had spent way too much time in the waiting room bored out of their minds, but some of them were genuinely good. He saw one very good rendition of a doctor giving a boy a lollipop done by Charles, a kid from Xander's neighborhood. Panning the wall a little more, he saw one by Chanelle McDonald, one without any blood, or anything else out of the ordinary on it anywhere. Just a girl playing with her cat, putting a red bow around its neck.

There was also a sketch there by Mandy.

"You like that one, huh?" Mandy asked, coming up behind him, her arms folded as she turned her head sideways and stuck out her tongue, sizing up the colouring of a boy and girl riding their bicycles down a country road from a different angle.

"A little prosaic for me, thanks," Xander said dryly, his eyes still darting over the wall, looking to see if there were any more by people he knew, like Kerri or Trina. "I prefer the work by the children five and under, usually the girls, but not exclusively. They just seem so much more creative. It's like modern art, except, done well."

"Life does mimic art," she said knowingly, nodding slowly.

He raised an eyebrow, turning toward her. "What's that supposed to mean?"

"I dunno," she shrugged, spinning around one full rotation before turning left and walking down the hall, Xander following her after another quick glance at the wall. "I heard it in a movie once, thought it sounded cool."

"Ah," he smiled, chuckling a little. "Very emulative of you."

"'Prosaic,' 'emulative'? What's up, did your Mom give you a word of the day calendar for your birthday or something?"

"Actually, yes. This month is descriptive words in sentences. What do you think?"

"I think you sound like a character from *Frasier*."

"Crap," he sighed, moving his mouth around as if he could place it somewhere different on his face, until it was finally a smile. "So, when were you in the hospital here?"

"Back when Mom was dating a real dick named Strickland. Guy took a hot clothes iron to the side of my face."

"Ouch."

"Yea. That's how I got that scar."

"Huh."

There was a silence between them then, and Mandy stopped walking, turning instead toward the door to their left. It was Julie's room door.

Several moments passed, in which they both stood, facing the door but not looking at it.

"You gonna go in, or are we admiring the paint on the door now?" Mandy asked, smiling from ear to ear as she leaned in front of Xander's blank face.

"I don't know if I can," he whispered, his lower lip shaky.

"Sure you can! You just turn the knob, push, and -"

"Not what I meant," he sighed, slumping his shoulders in frustration. "Can you come in with me?"

"Absolutely not," she replied, with no hint of her usual humor.

"What?"

"This is not one of those things I can play audience for," she said, then turned and walked toward the cafeteria. "I'll be around after if you need me, kay?"

"You always are," he smiled, watching her go until she was around the corner.

Taking a deep breath, he turned the knob and entered the room.

A nurse looked up at him, a brief look of shock on her face as she finished snapping in a fresh bag of clear liquid into the top of Julie's IV.

"Oh," she said, simply, blushing slightly as she was taken off guard. "I'm sorry, I wasn't expecting her to have any more visitors today."

"More?" Xander poised, raising an eyebrow.

"Yes, that nice boy from town Tommy Irons was in to

see her earlier, but she wasn't awake. She still isn't now, but you can sit with her if you're very quiet."

Xander nodded, then stepped into the room, sighing as he saw the almost worried expression on Julie's face as she slept. She looked as though she were very uncomfortable.

"Do I... know you?" The nurse asked as she passed by him, turning her head and giving him a slight smile. "I've seen you around here, haven't I? I'm Nurse Reilly."

"Hmm," Xander hummed, moving forward without paying so much as a seconds attention to the woman before she shrugged and walked out. He moved to her bedside, sniffling back a sinus full of mucus, then reached out his hand and touched hers, holding it tightly. He gazed at her beautiful face, so white and flushed out, willing the colour to return to it quickly, and just for him.

But it didn't, and it wouldn't.

"Come on, Jules," he coaxed, shaking her hand a little, sighing. "I don't know why I'm here," he admitted finally. "You've made it pretty clear that you don't want to be my girlfriend anymore. I'm pretty sure that if you actually did wake up with me next to you like this you'd slap me and call security or something to that effect... I just need to know that you're going to be okay. I rounded up all the Tees, I... I'm doing everything I can to try and make things better and it's just not..."

He looked at her longingly, then sat down at the chair next to her, buried his face in her sheets, and began to weep.

CHAPTER SIXTEEN
CRASHING

Trina sat before them both as they stood over her, both of their arms crossed.

Mike and Cathy both glared down at her little sister, anger and astonishment in their eyes as she tried to evaluate what she should say next.

"I'm... really sorry?" She said, flashing her brightest, toothiest smile as she fixed the shoulder of her top from coming down her arm.

"Oh, you have no idea," Mike fumed, his nostrils flaring.

"John Stein?" Cathy asked for the third time, raising an eyebrow in disbelief, trying to stop herself from laughing.

"Yeah?" Trina responded, almost defensively.

"Didn't we used to call him Hubble?" She asked, turning to Mike.

"Yeah," Mike smiled coyly, nodding. "He had lenses so big they looked like the Hubble Space Telescope."

"Right. Guy was like Piggy from *Lord of the Flies* all

through High School, from what I recall."

Trina rolled her eyes, fumbling with her fingers on her knee, looking around the kitchen for anything that would captivate her attention so that she wouldn't have to face their icy stares again.

"Hey," Mike said, calling the girl's attention back to him. "Are we boring you? Because if we are, I'm sure your folks could come home and find a way to keep you entertained."

"Oh no, Mike, please... you wouldn't..." she pleaded, whining.

"But I would," Cathy corrected, stepping forward and leaning in at the same time, trying to be as menacing as she could be. "I thought you'd learned from my mistakes, and then you go running off with an older guy in the woods and take your clothes off? What were you thinking?"

"She wasn't," Mike snickered. "It's a Kennessy family trait."

"Shut up," Cathy spat, forcing back laughter as she shot him a look, then turned back to her sister. "If you ever do anything like this again, Trean... you won't have to worry about Mom and Dad, because they'll have to put you back together to deal with you after I'm done."

Trina swallowed hard, never once breaking eye contact with her sister.

"Because I love you, and I would rather destroy you than watch you do it to yourself," Cathy added, snorting air through her nose for effect. She turned to Mike, cocking her head toward the door. "Go check out that dog she's so worried about."

Mike nodded, getting up and walking out their back

doors, heading off into the woods.

Cathy turned to her sister. Slowly, a smile crept over her lips, until it spread from ear to ear. "He is quite a dish, isn't he?"

Trina smiled.

Mike walked out into the woods, following the footprints in the slush that Trina and John had made. Smiling and shaking his head, he thought of the very similar thing that had almost happened between him and Cathy back at the house.

I'm not ready for that again, he thought, pushing past a tree branch. *I mean, I love her and I want to be with her, in every way… but after everything that happened last time, I just wonder if it's worth the risk to hurt her, or to hurt the two of us that way again. And if it's not worth the risk… why are we even together?*

He bent down and picked up Trina's bra off the ground, rolling his eyes and shoving it into his jacket pocket and trying to imagine what would be the most embarrassing way to give it back to her.

The footprints veered left and traveled over a log, so he hopped over it. Glancing around, he saw it. All of it. The dog, strewn out as though it were being sliced open for a meal, parts of it taken out, examined, and then tossed aside, as if uninteresting. There was blood everywhere, along with a stench that was unmatched to any dead thing he had ever been close to in his life, like blood and feces and wet dog all rolled into one. He balked, turning away quickly.

Then he stopped, glancing back at the beast, his eyes growing wide.

"Aw, no," he whispered, turning and running back toward the house as fast as he could, the bra dropping out of his pocket again as he went.

CHAPTER SEVENTEEN
WAKEUP

Xander stirred, waking up laid back in the chair next to Julie's bed. She was still asleep, and at some point it had gotten dark out. He looked around quickly, then checked his skin for the familiar feeling of dried blood. Finding none, he breathed a deep sigh of relief, then relaxed back in the chair again.

Julie was still in the same position she had been when he had cried himself to sleep, laid back with her hands outstretched, her face as white as a ghost with the clear expression of pain on it.

He gazed at her, sighed, then slammed his hands against the armrests of the chair and got up. He marched toward the door, cursing under his breath as he went. When his hand touched the knob he stopped, his eyes softening, and he turned and took a step back toward her.

Leaning over her bed, he gave her the smallest, softest kiss possible on her lips, never once closing his eyes. He turned back, opened the door, and exited the room.

Sweat poured off him as the room seemed to sway this

way and that, like the deck of a boat during rough seas. He thought he might throw up, so he leaned against the wall to wait for the feeling to pass.

"Jeez, you look like crap," Mandy smiled, chomping down on a Butterfinger bar as she walked toward him. She peeled the wrapper down a little more and took a large bite that sent flakes of clustered peanut brittle sprinkling to the floor around her.

"Don't hold back..." he smirked, his voice gruff and sickly. "...Tell me how you really feel."

"Don't worry, I always do." She smiled perkily, grabbing his arm and throwing it over her shoulder to help him walk. "The Womb's healing factor still hasn't helped much, huh?"

He shot her a glare. He hated it when she brought up that she knew about the Womb, especially in public, wishing that it hadn't flowed off him when he saved her from the Tees a few weeks ago.

"No, it hasn't," he answered, when it became clear that she wasn't about to accept his glare as a viable response. "Mike had this theory the other day that the Womb may not have the antibodies to properly deal with what's in me."

"So...like, in that case, you just, like, swallowed toxic bacteria, and you'll handle it just like I would?"

"I doubt that's actually the case," he smiled, hearing the concern in her voice. "Before we met, on one of my first times out as the Womb, I got into an explosion out on the highway. It was bad stuff. The Womb wouldn't even turn on for almost two weeks."

"Weird," she drawled, shoving her candy bar into his

face. "Want a bite?"

He stared at it for a long moment, then at her. "No," he said finally, starting to walk on his own again. "No, I don't. Why are you still here, anyway?"

"Waiting for you," she said in a cheery, matter-of-fact voice, popping up next to him and putting her arm around his.

He paused a moment at that, looking at her in a different light.

The both of them stopped for a moment, turning into the children's ward.

Xander opened the door, and a few of the children looked up to see who was coming in, but not many. His gaze fell over the room, until finally coming upon the empty bed of Chanelle McDonald.

His brow furrowed.

"What?" Mandy asked, her gaze following his. "Oh, right. That girl you helped. She's gone. She got sent home while you were out playing sick."

"Wasn't playing," he corrected.

"I know, but it sounds funny."

"Really doesn't."

She pouted, finished off her candy bar and then tossed the wrapper into a nearby trashcan. "What's the big deal? She's fine."

"I know. I just wanted to see her."

Mandy gave him a slack-jawed look for a moment, and then promptly closed her mouth, looking away at an assortment of "Get Well Soon" cards along a pegboard.

"Oh," she said, trying not to look too disappointed.

He turned, grinning at her. "But now I'm glad she's not

here, because now I get to spend more time with you."

She smiled, her features becoming soft, then she turned back toward the door and started walking away, hiding her face from him.

"Actually, I've got to go," Mandy said, wiping something from her eye. "I, um, I promised Aunt Sam that I'd call her and tell her how Julie's doing, y'know?"

"Yeah," Xander groaned as he watched her leave the room. "Sure."

He turned back toward Chanelle's bed, reaching under it and pulling out her colouring book. A bemused expression came over him as he flicked through it page by page, watching the artwork as it steadily progressed into happier, healthier things, until the last page, which was torn out. He assumed that had been the page that he had seen posted on the wall outside.

"What are you doing?" Came a voice from the doorway.

The voice brought Xander out of the hypnotic state he'd placed himself in, and he quietly pushed the book back under the bed, turning to smile at Mike. "Nothing much. What are you doing here?"

Mike gave him a look, both tired and saddened and angry.

"What?" Xander asked again, rising to his feet. "What is it?"

CHAPTER EIGHTEEN
GHOSTS OF THE PRESENT

"And you're sure?" Xander asked again, as he, Mike and Cathy marched down the street as fast as they could without seeming suspicious to the passerby. A few hours earlier and they would have gotten looks from behind every window, but people in this part of town shied away from looking out their windows at night. Too often, they saw something they wished they hadn't.

Again, Mike shot him a glare.

Cathy frowned, unable to hide the intense worry on her face, eyes sparkling with newly shed tears. "A poor dog, and now a murder? What else could it be, Xander?"

"Any number of things," Xander contested, his shoulders slumping in defeat.

They still hadn't said it yet. Neither of them wanted to, neither of them would dare. It was as if they were in some cheesy horror movie where simply saying the creature's name would draw it out.

"It's Zakron," Mike blurted finally, the name slicing deep into each of them like a knife. "It fits his profile. Animal deaths, and now Jesse Larkin? I saw him in the hospital before I came down and got you, man. He was ripped to shreds. There is no way anything but that monster did this."

Cathy didn't say anything, just kept her head down and stared at the sidewalk below her feet.

"The Anti-Womb," Xander grumbled, running his nails through his hair. The veins in his eyes had become varicose from his sickness and the sudden rise in blood pressure since hearing the name. "Last time I saw that thing, it was getting carted away by Circe."

"But you beat Circe," Mike said. "So this is how they're getting their revenge?"

"We should call Megan," Cathy said in a neutral tone of voice, eyes still glued to the pavement. "Last time it went after Adam. She could up the security around his room."

Xander pointed at her, affirming her suggestion. "Right," he agreed, turning to Mike. "And we need to get busy. We need to know how to fight this thing or we are screwed. The Womb's out of commission, and Zakron is always ready to party."

Mike nodded, then looked up, as if a light were going off in his head.

"O'Toole," he said, slapping Xander on the arm, as if to scold them both for not thinking of it sooner. "He released Zakron the last time. He must have files on him in his old office. All we gotta do is break in there and they're ours."

Xander smiled slyly. "Good idea."

"I was overdue."

"Guys..." Cathy said, stopping dead in her tracks, her body ridged and stiff.

"What is it?" Mike asked, his voice going from stone hard to completely soft as he touched her face, stroking it gently. "What's wrong?"

Xander looked around, his nostrils flaring as he sucked back snot and spit it out, trying to clear his sinuses. He turned, seeing the top of the mall peeking over the roofs of houses one street over. "Mike," he asked, looking at the long drag marks going down the sidewalk. "Didn't you say that the murder was around here somewhere?"

Cathy pointed to a bush, then collapsed into Mike's arms. "It's going to happen again," she whispered, stroking his chest. "We were thinking about it and now it's going to happen again, all of it."

"No, baby..." Mike said, eyes growing wide as he saw what she saw by the bush. "...Xander?"

"Yeah?" Xander asked, nose twitching as he turned back toward them. He followed both their gazes to the base of the bush, where the body of a small tabby cat lay skinned.

"There's a joke there, but it's just too easy." Xander sighed, his nostrils flaring again.

"Do you smell something?" Mike asked, taking a step toward him.

"I thought your senses were dulled back?" Cathy questioned, moving with her boyfriend, not wanting to let go of his arms.

"They are," he assured them, looking toward the house that the bush belonged to, "But I'd never miss that smell, not once you know it."

"What's that?"

"Fear," he said, curling his lips with disgust as they all looked at the name on the mailbox.

It read: McDonald.

Xander stepped back a little, retracting the hand he had extended toward the child's activity book. "Okay. That's... that's okay," he said soothingly, crumpling his forehead. He glanced down at the girl's arms, seeing them bruised and swollen, her legs larger than normal as well. He sighed, then got up to walk away.

"So, what do we do?" Mike asked, rubbing Cathy's shoulders as she finally stopped crying.

"Just what we planned to," Xander growled, clenching his teeth so hard that they ground together.

ʎʕʎ

Xander pulled his hand back out of the broken window of Dr. Warren O'Toole's office, grimacing as the glass cut into his flesh. He motioned to Mike, who rolled his eyes before reaching through the smashed glass and unlocked the door, opening it.

On the floor, the letters of the good Doctor's name were scattered about and rearranged. It made Mike smile, just a little.

"You break, I enter. We make an excellent team," he said, looking around the dark of the office.

Xander stared at the open wounds on his hand as the blood drained down them. Slowly, the wounds stopped bleeding and began to close, at a tenth of their usual rate, making it much longer and more excruciating, like the glass was being ripped through each cell individually.

Mike moved over to a filing cabinet, then opened it and started flicking through the papers. A queer look came over him as he lifted one file out and opened it.

"What is that?" Xander asked, sniffing and grunting as his hand finally pushed out the last few slivers of glass.

"It's Mandy Peterson's file," Mike said absent-mindedly, not taking his eyes off the page.

Xander shook his head. "Do you really think Warren would be stupid enough to keep his Circe folders here, in an unlocked cabinet? They're probably in his loft."

"We'll have to make a point of retrieving them," Mike resolved, snapping the file shut and putting it back in the cabinet, flicking through some more until he found what they were looking for. "Here we go. Chanelle McDonald."

Xander leaned over his shoulder, reading the file along with him. "Says here she came to school every few weeks with fresh bruises, the last time so bad that the school remanded her to the hospital."

"Look at this," Mike said, pointing to an entry near the top of the page. "Chanelle and her family only moved here three months ago. Before that they were living in Indigo, Utah. There was a fire at the house, with Chanelle trapped inside. Firefighters found bars on her windows and her door locked from the outside. Before that, the McDonalds lived in Oregon, where neighbors and a family member were found murdered. The deaths were never solved."

Xander glared at the file photo of Chanelle, one of her eyes black, ruining her beautiful face.

"We need to see that body," he said decisively, turning toward the door as Mike put the file back.

⋏⋎⋏

Chanelle McDonald lifted her mug of hot chocolate to her lips and took an enjoyable sip, several tiny melted marshmallows squiggling down her throat as she did. She smacked her lips together dramatically, like the child on the commercials for grape juice, and exclaimed: "Ah!"

At the end of the table, her father looked up and glared at her. He squinted hard, and then slowly turned his attention back toward his paper, scanning through the business section.

Chanelle's gaze lowered, a frown spreading across her lips as she brought the cup of hot chocolate back up to them and guzzled down the last of it.

"Okay," her father said, putting down the paper and stepping toward her. "You've had your treat, now it's time for bed."

"No!" Chanelle cried defiantly, a touch a fear in her voice as she jerked away from him.

He reached out and grabbed her arm so fast that she barely saw it coming, as though he'd been sitting in one frame of her mind's reel and then on her the next. Standing, he dragged her through the hallway and opened the door to her bedroom, forcing her inside and then finally letting her go. There were red lines on her arm from where his hand had been.

She spun and clacked her teeth at him as though she could bite him from across the room, her cheeks flushed with red. "No!" She screamed again, as though he hadn't already forced her inside.

He slammed the door even as she was protesting and

turned the padlock on it with his thumb. It slid into place with a firm *cl-clack* before he slid his hand down further and found a second padlock, sliding it into place as well. *Cl-clack*. Finally his hand fell upon the key that rested in the doorknob and turned it all the way around. When he heard the mechanism inside click, he put the key in his pocket and walked back down the hallway. Returning to the table he picked up his paper again. The Mets had won.

"Get out of the way," one doctor screamed, waving for both of them to move. Julie jumped up right away, but Mike stayed there, still as a marble statue, looking down at the woman he loved as blood poured from his body, but he paid it no mind. It was of no consequence to him.

He was pushed out of the way and backed up a few steps silently, as two men laid a stretcher out between him and his love. They hoisted her up onto it, and immediately the clean, white sheet turned to dark red. Blood seeped out from between her legs, and she did not move. Never once did she move. He reached out and touched her hand, and it was chilled, her lips blue.

Soft
Lime
Tender
Moist
Wet
stop.

"She's so cold," he said in a hollow voice, as he watched them wheel her away into the back of an ambulance. Julie slowly walked up behind him, reaching out and grasping his hand, then

wrapping both arms around him, bawling into his shirt. He turned to her, surprised that she was there, having not noticed her before. He stroked the back of her head, his stare falling past her at the rubble at their feet. "Should we get her a blanket?"

Cathy awoke with a start, her head numb after so much time pressed up against the library desk. She groaned as the blood rushed to her head, wondering how long she had been asleep for. Groggily, she turned her head (with one eye partially closed) to the clock on the wall, and realized that she had missed gym. Stopping to think about her schedule for a minute, she realized that she had Family Education with Miss Waller again now. Thinking back on her performance at their last class, she decided against attending.

Soft
Lime
Tender
Moist
Wet

She blinked twice, and the thought vacated her head again. She sighed, slumped her head on one hand, reached to the nearest book, and opened it. She winced, trying to force the thought not to come back.

What if it happens again? What if I get pregnant again? I can't put Mike through that. I just can't. Oh gawd... what are we doing...

She sighed again, pulling the book closer to her, getting out of her own light, and trying to immerse herself into the literature.

CHAPTER NINETEEN
VIVISECTION

Harry Ford took a deep bite of his chicken sub, the honey mustard on it dripping down from the bottom in huge yellow dollops that splattered against the wax paper in his lap. He stifled a laugh as the cartoon duck on the screen in front of him slammed into a wall, then peeled himself off as though he had no more substance than a Post-It Note .

Lance snarled at him, shaking his head. "I don't know how you can watch that."

Harry wiped his mouth in his sleeve. "I get one, one lunch break. I'll spend it how I please."

"The screen is so small."

"It's a phone."

"But... still."

Harry rolled his eyes and then went back to his meal.

Lance continued to poke at his fruit cup idly, curling his lip at the chunk of red sponge that was in it. He wasn't sure what it had been in life, but now it had just absorbed the tastes of everything that had been around it, coming out as a mix of cherry and banana. He wondered if it had actually been a sponge.

Around the corner, Mike took a deep breath, then continued counting down.

"Ninety-eight, ninety-seven, ninety-six..."

He wasn't counting down to anything per se, it was just something he'd discovered helped calm him. The numbers helped bring some order and focus to the chaos around him.

He wondered, briefly, if he would grow up to be an accountant.

He then wondered if he would live to grow up at all. That thought stayed with him, even as he raised the cheap Bic lighter he'd lifted from Xander up to the sprinkler head above him and struck the flint. Fire shot out, moving smoothly over the metal surface.

Nothing happened.

He stood there and stared at it for a long moment, until the top of the lighter got so hot that he thought it would burn his hand.

"Dammit!" He yelled, then punched the wall next to him. It made a loud, heavy thud.

Harry looked up from his sandwich. "Did you hear that?"

Mike's face went white. He turned around quickly and made his way for the stairwell.

"Sounded like something dropped..." Lance answered, even as he got up and started walking down the hall.

Harry followed, and they both rounded the corner just in time to see the stairwell door close. "Hey!" He yelled, and the both of them bolted for the door, trying the handle and finding that it was locked. "Hey! Let us in!" They banged on the door fiercely.

Around the opposite side of the stairwell, Mike came around the corner. Tiptoeing, he made his way to the morgue entrance and ducked inside.

"Are we there yet?" Mandy whined, rolling her eyes as she walked alongside Xander, her pigtails bobbing up and down on either side of her head like little pom-poms.

"Yes!" Xander hissed at her, pointing to the house they were standing in front of. "Yes, this time, we are actually here. Not like the first five hundred and fifty times you asked."

Mandy gave him a look, taking one last suck of her popsicle before tossing it into the bushes next to the house. "I really don't think it was that many times. You're greatly exaggerating your math here, boy-o."

"Boy-o?" He repeated, raising an eyebrow at her.

"I always call you boy-o."

"Never once in your life have you called me boy-o. I mean, ever. Ev! Er!"

"Oh," Mandy clicked her tongue, eyes darting to one side, away from him. "Maybe that's just from one of the conversations I had with you in my head and didn't out loud."

"You have conversations with me... in your head."

"Uh-huh."

"Yeah, and I'm the weird one."

"No, you're the boy-o. Say it with an Irish accent. It's fun."

He stopped, turning to glare at her.

"Words fail me," he groaned, starting up the path to the house of Lindsey McDonald. "What are you doing here anyway? I'm going after a child-beater. Probably not the safest mission for you to accompany me on. Besides, everyone knows Mike's my sidekick."

"I think you're his sidekick."

"I'm the one with powers, so he's my sidekick."

"I think it takes more than--"

"I'm the one with powers, so he's my sidekick."

"Touched a nerve, have I?"

"My last one," he growled, knocking on the white, metal door, then ringing the door bell. "Seriously, Mandy, you shouldn't be here. You could get hurt, and if anything happened to you..." his voice got quiet suddenly, as he looked away from her. "...Your cousin would never forgive me."

The door opened suddenly, and Lindsey McDonald loomed a good two feet over him, glaring down.

"What do you want?" He said in a gruff voice. A blind man could have told that he was from Utah with that accent. He wasn't necessarily strong looking, just very tall and broad. He was unshaven and his eyes and nose were red, either from excess alcohol or not enough sleep. Or both. He looked like the type of person that could snap at any given moment, in Xander's experience.

And I should know, we can smell our own.

"Um..." Xander stammered, eyes widening. "Me and my friend here were just going to talk to you about, um, about Jesse Larkin. If that's alright." He turned to motion to Mandy, discovering that she had taken his advice and left. Oh yeah, that makes me look real good, he sighed, then turned back to the man.

"What about Chanelle's sitter?" Lindsey asked, leaning in and raising an eyebrow.

"He's... dead?" Xander said slowly, sizing the man up and down.

Sweat immediately began to pour down the man's brow, as he stood back from the door to let Xander inside.

Cathy sat back with the large brown bound book in front of her, resting comfortably on her legs. She flipped through it aimlessly, not looking for anything in particular but becoming more and more interested the more she discovered.

There were dozens of articles on the Salem witch trials and myths about ogres and werewolves from the eighteenth century. She stopped at a section on Dracula's connection to Vlad the Impaler, winced at an etching of a silhouetted man impaled on a spike, then turned the page.

The Boogey Man that Xander had fought looking back at her, grotesque smile and all.

She jerked back a bit, a shudder traveling down her spine so powerful that she almost dropped the book. She turned the page to get away from it, then stopped.

Sitting up straight, she flipped back to the text on the Ok' La' Zarr.

Her eyes grew wide. She got up from her desk and ran for the door as fast as she could.

⋔

The metal shelf opened with a clang. Mike put his hand on the cloth covering Jesse Larkin's body.

He shivered. The cold, sterile environment of the coroner's office bit at his skin. Steeling himself for something he knew would be unseemly, he pulled back the cloth to reveal Larkin's entire form. Holding his breath, he forced himself to look at the punctuated remains of Larkin's stomach. It was covered in nearly identical, sharp little holes. They looked like mouths.

He let out the breath he'd been holding and brought one gloved hand up, pulling at the skin on Jesse's stomach to open the wound. He started to count again.

The wounds were slanted downward, their tracts leading toward the more extensive wounds around his pelvis.

He stopped counting, even in his head.

A curious look came over him, and he bent down to one of the stab wounds just above Larkin's penis. There were chunks of denim fibers caught in it from where he'd been stabbed through his jeans.

The wounds were the same as before, the tracts slanted downward.

His brow furrowed. He turned around and walked toward the far wall where a model of a skeleton stood erect. Imagining that the dummy was Jesse, he stood next to it, clutching his tweezers as one would a knife or dagger.

Holding the "handle" firmly he stabbed Jesse in the lower gut. Looking down at where the tweezers entered the model, he saw that they slanted upwards, toward the head. He tried several more times from different angles, but the result was the same, the knife, and wound tract, would have to be pointing upwards.

A haggard look slowly came over Mike's face, his muscles relaxing, as he knelt down onto both knees, swinging the "knife" over his head to strike, coming into contact with Jesse Larkin's abdomen, the tweezers pointing down, toward his crotch.

He stopped, thinking about what he had just discovered. *Concealment? Maybe he was knelt in a bush when he struck, or...* he stopped, his eyes growing wide as he scrambled to his feet and ran for the door as fast as his legs would carry him.

CHAPTER TWENTY
JERUSALEM

"God, I'm so sorry..." Lindsey gasped, sitting down at his kitchen table again. He held his head in his hands as tears started to dribble down his cheeks, dotting onto the newspaper below, still spread out to the sports section from the night before.

Well, this is a new one on me. Xander frowned, watching as the man broke down from the simple confrontation of hearing his victim's name.

"There was blood," he said, looking at Xander and then turning away. "Oh, my gawd, there was so much blood."

"Jesse's blood," Xander said, completing the thought as Lindsey seemed incapable of getting a full one out. "That is what you're saying... right?"

"I tried forever to get it out. It just wouldn't come clean, it wouldn't... couldn't..."

"Yeah..." Xander sighed. "It never comes out easy."

"I swear..." he moaned, his body racked with sobs. "I swear I didn't mean to, I was just trying to protect my family..."

"How the hell were -" Xander started, growing more and more confused by the second.

The phone rang, startling them both.

Xander turned to Lindsey, who just continued to sit there and weep.

"Yeah, sure, I'll get it then," he said under his breath, walking to the far wall and picking up the receiver. "Hello?"

"Xander!?" Cathy screamed frantically into the other end, followed by a sigh of relief.

"Cathy?" He spat, whispering now, turning his back to Lindsey. "What are you doing calling here -"

"You have to get out of there!" Cathy screamed into the other end, panic taking over her voice again. "You have to leave, now!"

"Cathy, what are you talking about?"

"The Ok' La' Zarr... it's a body jumper!"

"What?"

There was pain then, a blinding white pain that took over his entire field of vision. It was accompanied by a hollow ringing sound and continued to gong like a bell even after the blow had been struck.

Xander hit the floor hard, his face beating off the edge of the wall, sending blood and mucus in all directions. He rolled over as his sinuses clogged, his vision getting hazy, just in time to see Chanelle raise her father's baseball bat again...

Another loud smack echoed through the house, and for a moment Xander thought he'd been hit again. The world spun around in front of him, but Chanelle still stood there. Her eyes were alight with rage and she was wearing a grin so wide it showed off all of her round, tiny teeth right to the gums. The bat hadn't come down though, and she turned and hissed at something he couldn't see.

He tried to turn and his whole world shifted to the right.

There was another loud crash as the wood around the McDonald's deadbolt finally splintered and Mike fell into the house, stumbling once and catching himself. His eyes locked to Xander's only briefly when he saw Chanelle, her arms raised as she held the bat taller than her into the air.

"Okay, kid," he coaxed, holding out his hand and stepping toward the child cautiously. "Why don't you just give me the bat, and then we'll get you some double-fudge-mint-chip ice cream or something, huh? You in the mood for a sugar..."

There was a groan to his side, and Mike turned to see Lindsey McDonald laying on the floor beside the couch. There were two other pairs of feet poking out from behind it as well. One was clearly a child's. The other wore heels.

"...rush," he finished, turning back to her.

She grinned at him, and then swung the bat. It slammed it into Mike's side with more force than she should have been capable of and sent him stumbling across the room and into the far wall. Two pictures and a vase fell off a nearby shelf down onto him as he landed on the hard-wood floor, feeling something in his tailbone bend to the point of breaking then go back again.

"Ah!" He hissed through his teeth, closing his eyes tight as pain ripped through his body from several points and all converged on his skull as if on a race.

Xander's eyes opened suddenly, his face blank of all expression. Something deep inside of him twitched once, and then again.

Groggily, Mike opened his eyes. Chanelle was standing over him, her bat gripped tight between both hands. Her hair was wild and out of control, sticking out in all directions. Her cheeks had become crystalline, bloodshot and shiny, like dried flakes of desert dotting her face. Her eyes were no longer there... instead there were dual black holes, gaping maws that seemed to stretch on for eternity. He gasped, even as she drew back the bat again and brought it down across his face, sending him sprawling into the couch, a quick spurt of blood splashing onto the dark fabric.

The veins in Xander's eyes became prominent, making them red and bulging for a moment. That thing deep in him twitched and his eyes went quickly from red to a thick black. He rose quickly to his feet as the gash on the side of his face healed, sewing itself back up until there was nothing there but smooth skin.

He grabbed Chanelle by the back of the throat, turned her around, and slammed her against the wall just as she was about to strike Mike for a third time.

"Boo."

He tightened his grip on the possessed child's neck as the rest of the family started to stir and Mike ran to their aid, blood streaming down an impact wound on his own head as well. His ear was bleeding heavily.

Xander let his claws out of two of his fingers, puncturing the girl's neck just a little as he squeezed. She tried to scream, but found that she could not get enough air. Suddenly, her demonic eyes began to glow.

Xander's own blackened eyes widened, even as he continued to tighten his grip.

Something shoved Xander back as the room filled with light.

Chanelle dropped to the ground, coughing violently, holding her throat as tiny droplets of blood started to flow down it.

The light faded quickly and the Ok' La' Zarr stood there, looking dazed, its muscle tone slightly more green than it had been before. It looked less graceful, and its erection was gone as well. It screamed a high-pitched wail that made Xander cover his ears, his enhanced senses returning quickly.

"Discani!" It spat angrily. It took off toward the door and ripped it off its hinges as it passed.

Xander stammered to his feet and bolted over to Mike.

"It's corporeal," he said, helping the mother to her feet. "We can end this now."

"You go!" Mike nodded, taking the son onto his shoulder. "I'll take care of things here!"

Xander got up and ran toward the door as fast as he could, the Womb blood already coursing through his veins, waiting for the release, the pressure in his body building and building. As soon as he was out of earshot of the house, he bellowed "Black Womb lives," the reverberations of which came back at him almost immediately, attracting the attention of several dogs within a block of him.

"What was that thing?" Chanelle's mother exclaimed

as she rose to her feet, aided by Mike. "What the hell is going on here?"

"They know, Mary," Lindsey barked, sighing as he hoisted his son onto one arm. He walked over to where their daughter still knelt, coughing. He grimaced as she looked up at him, her eyes pale and innocent. "They know what she's done."

"Wait," Mike said as he sat down on the couch, smearing his own blood onto his jeans accidentally. "It wasn't her. That... thing you saw, it was like... a parasite. It was inside her, acting through her."

Lindsey furrowed his brow, as his daughter smiled up at him, leaping up into his arms. Fresh tears spilled down his cheeks, as his smile spread from ear to ear, the way it hadn't since all this began.

Mike smiled, laying back against a cushion and clutching his side. He watched as the father held his daughter as tightly as he dared, squeezing her as though he had not seen her in years.

⁀⟨⋏

The Ok' La' Zarr ran through the woods, shoving past trees and shrubs as it went, sweat beading on its skinless brow. It glanced behind its shoulder, breathing hard as it struggled to see if it was still back there, following him. Trying to see if it was still coming to get him. Fear washed over the fear demon's face, a look that didn't quite fit it, though the poetic nature of it would have been noticed by anyone who had been around to see it for what it was.

Its teeth ached with the cold winter air that flew around it in all directions, stinging its large, unprotected canines, like the feeling one gets when they drink cold juice. Its suit was torn and ripped by the foliage all around it. Deep inside its lanky chest its heart thumped loudly, sending blood coursing through its veins faster and faster until it thought that its head might explode.

It had never seen anything like that... thing... before. Never in its long life had it ever been touched by something so black, so dark. Never.

He looked over his shoulder again, then turned back to the front, slamming face first into the Black Womb and falling backward to the ground, scuffing its pants on the muddy, half-frozen ground.

"Take me not back there you can!" The creature hissed angrily, letting a glob of spit hanging from his mouth finally fall to his chest.

The Womb stepped toward it, not speaking. Not taking its large, red eyes off it.

"Not you can!" It bellowed again. It dove at the Womb with incredible speed, its hands spread wide and its long talons all seeming to point at him at once.

The Womb brought its hands up to defend itself as the creature plunged forward into it, then vanished into vapor.

A ripple of gooseflesh traveled over the Womb's black flesh, covering him in that same pins-and-needles feeling one got when a limb lay pinned for some time.

Xander turned around, fists still raised, trying to see where it had gone.

He grunted, feeling something drip onto his foot. When he looked there was a growing puddle of thick black soup growing between his feet and the Womb-flesh melted off of him. Fresh, human blood started to come out from his nose. He brought his hand up to catch it then held it up, confused at how much there was. It coated his fingers and palm in thick crimson, as though he were wearing some satin glove.

"What the hell?" he coughed gruffly. Pain erupted from his head like a massive migraine and his hands jolted up to clutch either side of it. It felt like his brain was ripping itself it two. "Oh... fuck."

It was dark.

Darker than it had ever seen, ever known in all its years. There was nothing for its senses to find there but the slow, methodic dripping of its own blood as it leaked from its veins. The demon took several slow steps to the right, gazing all around him with those eyes of nothing as it did.

Chills ran up and down its partially exposed spine as it explored its environment, unsure of what to make of it. It growled deep within its throat. Somewhere in the dark it thought it heard a child's whimper.

The Inner Child.

It smiled grotesquely, stepping forward and licking its lips with a long, sick tongue. It stepped toward the voice, looking from side to side for it, ready to pounce at a moment's notice. Drool salivated from his gums as it anticipated what it would be like, the first bites of the flesh and the final beats of the heart.

"Come outs..." it hissed, smiling as warm as a thing with a face like that could. "You have nothing to fear..."

Suddenly, two aqua eyes opened in the maw that surrounded it, glowing brightly as if from nothing.

The creature balked in shock as the Womb stepped out of the shadows toward it, opening up a full row of teeth.

"Make me go back you won't!" It screamed, lunging at the Womb.

It was batted away carelessly as the Womb opened up its mouth, bellowing at the very top of its lungs: "Black Womb lives!"

The Womb grabbed the demon by the head and snapped its spine with one skillful slice of its massive claws, paralyzing it.

Tears streamed down the demon's face as it tried to hold out its hands to block the Womb from coming toward it, but found itself unable to. All it could do was watch as the creature slowly slunk toward it, blue-green eyes large and unblinking.

"Didn't expect this, did you?" Xander snarled, blood gushing out his nose, ears and mouth as the last of the Womb seeped off his naked body and into the snow. "Trying to take me over you'll have to step in line."

It screamed as the true Womb leapt upon it, its massive jaw unhinging and growing to envelope the Ok' La' Zarr's entire body, swallowing one section at a time like an anaconda.

"The human, that's the part you like," Xander laughed, even as he began to even cry blood. "The Womb... that's a different story now, ain't it?"

It screamed, only its head remaining visible as it bawled for life, its eyes watching as the Womb's mouth came over them, bringing new pitch to the blackness all around it... and then, slowly, it began to laugh.

"What's so funny?" Xander asked himself, lying down in the snow now, unable to move. "You won't be taking little girls away where you're going, y'know."

"I never has to go back..." it laughed, even as the Womb took it into itself. "I never has to go back there again. No control. No help. Trapped we was, trapped. Trapped by the prey."

Xander's eyes lit up as the creature finally stopped laughing, light fading from Xander's eyes as it died, finally.

M

Chanelle laid the book down on the bed for him to see.

Xander's eyes went wide. His hand trembled as he picked up the book.

What had originally been a boy in a hospital bed with one leg in a cast and a doctor coming in through the nearby door had been turned into the same boy with dark red smears dripping from his eyes, mouth and ears. The doctor had been coloured in black, making him look shadowy and evil.

M

He grinned as he passed by a wall full of pages from children's colouring books, each a different picture coloured by a different child patient. Most where incoherent scribbles by children who had spent way too much time in the waiting room bored out of their minds, but some of them were the genuinely good. He saw one very good rendition of a doctor giving a boy a lollipop done by Charles, a kid from Xander's neighborhood. Panning the wall a little more, he saw one by Chanelle McDonald, one without any blood, or anything else out of the ordinary on it anywhere. Just a girl playing with her cat, putting a red bow around its neck.

M

Mike's eyes grew wide as he saw what Cathy saw by the bush. "...Xander?"

"Yeah?" Xander asked, nose twitching as he turned back to-

ward them. He followed both their gazes to the base of the bush, where the body of a small tabby cat lay skinned.

∧∨∧

Just a girl playing with her cat, red blood around its neck.

"Oh..." Xander said softly, staring up at the sky as he laid back against the snow, his muscles refusing to move. "... my god."

∧∨∧

Lindsey McDonald took the last screw out of the lock on his daughter's door, smiling as he chucked it to Mike. "Done," he said, unable to contain his enthusiasm.

"Done," Mike smiled in return, tossing the lock in the bathroom garbage. "So you were locking her in to stop her from hurting things?"

"Broke my heart every time," he sighed, the smile still on his face, his eyes bright and glimmering.

"That's great," Mike chuckled. "That is so much better than the way I thought all this would turn out, you have no idea."

"And you're sure your friend can handle that thing?" He asked, a touch of concern in his voice.

"Yeah, no problem," Mike smiled, handing him the screwdriver, which he placed on a shelf near the bathroom door. "He can handle himself."

Lindsey nodded, still unsure of what to make of everything that had happened. "I just can't believe it... all the bad things that have happened over the last few years, all because of that creature somehow?"

Mike smiled, nodded... and then the smile slowly faded from his lips.

"Years?" He repeated, as the two of them turned the corner into the living room again. He grabbed Lindsey by the shoulder and started to turn him around. "Did you say years?"

Both men stopped quickly, eyes wide as they saw Lindsey's wife and son sprawled out on the floor again. Blood was hemorrhaging out of Mary's back. They were both covered in a viscous fluid that Mike recognized automatically.

He turned back down the hall just in time to see the bat swipe across his face again, connecting with his nose. He hit the ground hard, his eyes glazing over as he felt something splash over his legs. The smell got worse as his eyes started to close, just in time to see Chanelle McDonald put down the can of gasoline.

She smiled down at Mike, holding up a book of matches. "The boy said that if my family dies... I get a new one."

CHAPTER TWENTY-ONE
BURN

CH!

TCH!

CH!

Chanelle sighed, pouting out her lower lip as she tried to light match after match, throwing the useless sticks to the floor.

CH!

Cathy came into the house slowly, walking around the corner and into the living room, refusing to so much as blink to take her eyes off the child.

"Hi, Chanelle," she said, sweat pouring off her brow from the run she'd had trying to get to the house in time.

CH!

Chanelle struck another match, the last of the powder wearing off before it even got to spark. Indignant, she threw the useless stick of cardboard to the ground.

"Hi," Chanelle said warmly, taking a moment to smile up at Cathy before she ripped off another match and tried to ignite it.

TCH!

Cathy winced every time the sound occurred, staring at the matchbook and watching for that one spark that would send the situation up into flames.

"What are you doing?" Cathy asked, in the nicest tone of voice she could muster, brushing a strand of hair back behind her ear. She smiled even as she looked down at Mike, his lower half drenched in gasoline.

CH!

"I'm starting a fire," the girl said simply. "Then I can have a new family."

Cathy nodded. "Okay..." she said, taking a quick glance around the room and spotting the bat a few feet to one side. "Why do you think you need a new family, Chanelle, sweetie?"

"Oh, I know I do," she said, not so much as throwing a glance at Cathy. "I have to get a new one so they can make me happy, so I can do whatever I want."

TCHC!

"You know, you don't have to set a fire just to get a new family..." she coaxed, slowly stepping forward, moving just a little to the right with each step she took, toward the bat.

"Oh, I know," the child assured her, smiling. "Fire's just fun."

CH-isssss!

The flame lit up on the edge of one of the matches, and Cathy's eyes went wide, the spark caught in both her pupils. "Chanelle, no!" She screamed.

Chanelle looked at her finally, the child's smile gone.

"Don't tell me what to do!" She screamed, tossing the

match down onto her mother's gasoline-soaked dress.

Flames erupted all around, sucking all of the air of the room and filling it with smoke.

"No!" Cathy screamed, raising her hands to block against the flames. They spread quickly, the fire moving from point to point along the spots in the carpet where fuel had dripped, like a bright orange stone skipping across the water and making ripples as it went.

The baby boy began to scream, the shrill wail heard even above the roar of the fire. The fire sounded like a dragon and the flames that kissed the undersides of Cathy's arms were its molten teeth.

Her eyes began to water from the smoke and the heat. She had to force herself to open them, her every instinct telling her not to. She squinted past the hole that her arms made in front of her and saw Mike, lying unconscious on the floor not far from where Chanelle's mother lay.

His arm was on fire.

Her eyes went wide, the smoke and the humidity stinging at them.

She dove forward into the flames, past the orange wall that stretched up to stain the ceiling a deep charcoal black already. It felt as though she were inside an oven. The heat that had hit her like a wave a moment ago was now all around her, pressing in on her from all sides and making her feel as though she might implode. Her lungs ached for air but every breath brought more pain, the smoke searing her flesh on the way down like millions of tiny axes. She coughed, gasped for air and got more smoke, then coughed again.

Her hands found Mike's chest and she forced herself

to stop coughing. The wall of fire was dissected by her abdomen and seemed to have quelled the fire directly beneath it, a long doorway having opened in the flames all the way to the ceiling. She discovered now that the orange wasn't so much a wall but a large and ever-expanding box, within which was just more flames.

Her hair catching and filling the room with the disgusting and unmistakable stench of burnt hair, she grabbed him by his shoulder and the neck of his shirt and pulled with everything she had in one mighty tug, bringing him over to the other side of the fire.

She gasped for air from the exertion and immediately regretted it, her lungs rebelling wildly against the smoke and screaming in pain. Her vision blurred and large red dots decorated all sides of it. A migraine came out of nowhere, the first in her life, so blindingly painful that she clenched her teeth hard enough to crack a molar. Forcing herself not to faint, she kicked Mike in the ribs as hard as she could and sent him tumbling toward the front door, where he slammed against the jam and stayed there at an obtuse and painful angle. His mouth was open, his eyes were not.

His shirt was still on fire.

Pursing her dried and cracked lips, she turned back to the flame. Chanelle was still standing beyond it, her back to the wall. She looked at Cathy expectantly, the fire dancing in her glossy, moist eyes.

Closing her eyes, Cathy dove forward into the flames once again. She felt the tips of it against the skin of her chin. Her hand connected with hot fabric and she pulled back, throwing herself away from the fire with such force that she knocked her head against the doorframe and pushed Mike out of the house and onto the walkway.

The baby was clutched tightly to her chest.

"No!" Chanelle cried from the house, coughing as her little lungs filled with smoke. "You can't! I don't want you to!"

Cathy grabbed sand and dirt from the walkway and threw it against Mike's shoulder, burying not only that side of his face and torso but the fire as well. The ground she'd piled there smoked and smoldered like a volcano about to erupt.

"I don't want you to!"

The baby cried, finally able to again now that its lungs were filling with the night air.

Cathy turned back toward the house as flames engulfed the door she had just come through, making it impossible for her to get back in.

Firefighters arrived on the scene twenty minutes later, when the house and the three people remaining inside were nothing but piles of charred ruin.

EPILOGUE

"So... it was the kid all along?" Mandy asked, as she and Xander walked down the darkened sidewalk a few days later. The streetlight cast long shadows on each of them.

Xander nodded, taking a puff of his cigarette and then throwing it aside.

"That's so awful..." she trailed off, looking down at the sidewalk. "Give me a straight bad guy any day. This stuff, when you don't, like, know what's right and what's not... it's just too much. You know?"

"Yeah," Xander sighed, turning to smile at her briefly. "I do."

She smiled at him coyly, one eyebrow raised suspiciously. "So, where are you taking this innocent teenage girl on this cold winter's night that you can't tell me, anyway?"

"You're not innocent, by any stretch," Xander said, without humor, even though he meant for there to be.

She frowned, knowing full well what that tone in his

voice meant. "Hey... there was nothing that you could have done. You did your part... more than. Like always." She drew her hand in close to his cheek, tilting his head up to look at her. "I love you, boy-o."

Xander smiled as best he could, his eyes welling up. "I love you, too."

He turned off the main road then, heading up the path toward the cemetery.

"Hey, what're we going up here for?" Mandy asked, looking around cautiously, sweat beginning to dot on her brow even though she was shivering.

Xander did not answer, just continued to walk up the trail, with her no less than three paces behind him at all times.

"Xander, I don't like it up here," she whined, shivering again. "I'm cold, can we go please?"

Again, he said nothing. Tears started to draw forth from his eyes and he batted them free, trudging his way silently up the steep slope.

"Xander please, I don't want to -"

And then there was silence. Xander stood staring down at the grave before him. Engraved on the stone was the most beautiful name he thought he might ever hear : Amanda Peterson.

"Goodbye," he said softly, bowing his head.

Several long moments passed, and then someone else stepped up next to him again, gazing down at the grave with him.

"Hello, Alex," she said simply, her eyes pinned to the letters and date engraved into the stone.

"Hello, Julie," he sighed, touching her hand briefly.

"When did they let you out?"

"Few hours ago," she said, her voice and lower lip quivering, her face still a little flush. "I came here as soon as I could."

Xander nodded. Neither of them looked at the other.

"She was so brave," Xander said, his eyes getting red and puffy. "Oh, gawd, Julie, you should have seen it. She looked soooo pretty, she did, and her eyes were sparkling right up until the spark went out, I swear... nobody has ever seen anything so beautiful as her eyes right before it happened. It was like all the wonder that was meant for the rest of her life got crammed into that one second, and I was there to see it."

Julie nodded, tears dribbling from her chin as though it were a faucet. "It's good that someone was there with her," she said simply. "I just wish I knew why all this had to happen."

He opened his mouth and let it lay slack for a moment, then he pulled a knife from his jacket and brought it to his wrist behind his back.

"There's something I have to tell you," he whispered softly.

"Don't," she spat, taking him by surprise. "I mean... just don't." She looked down, sniffing back hard. "I'm going back to Coral Cove tomorrow, Xander."

"What?" He exclaimed, putting the knife away quickly.

"I can't do it anymore. And my Aunt needs me now, me and Mom. I asked her and we're both going now, so that she won't have to be alone anymore. It's for her, I just..." Again, she sucked back tears, turning to face him for the first time since she'd joined him. "I just can't keep competing with dead women."

He stepped back a pace, shocked.

"It's not Sara... it's not that you still love her, in ways you can't love me. That's not it, Xander. It's what you really love more than anything. You love *death*, Xander Drew... and as long as you do, death will keep following you, wherever you go, and I can't be a part of that anymore."

His lower lip quivered, so she reached out and kissed it, lightly. "I love you, Alexander Drew," she said, wiping tears from her face as she walked away from him, heading back down the hill into town.

In his room, Mike held Cathy close to him as they lay on his bed, looking up at the posters on his wall. He stroked her hair and just held her, as she snuggled up closer to him, fitting perfectly against his body.

"About... what we were talking about the other day..." he said slowly, kissing her on top of her head.

"Yeah?" She smiled, looking up at him longingly.

He sighed. "Everything's just so different. Everything's changing all at once again, and I don't know when it's going to stop. I just... I just want us, right now, to be the one place that I can go and know what to expect for once. I want us to change, to go to that next level..."

"...But not yet," she smiled, leaning up and kissing him, softly, on the lips. "I feel the same way."

He smiled, cuddling her close to him again, just staring up at the walls.

"In the darkness it followed them, just enough light for them to see. It chased them through the brush and the woods, the tree limbs scraping past them, tearing at their limbs, cutting deep, deep, everything cut deep. The wind whistled through the branches as they ran past, singing the songs of their deaths, and it was beautiful.

"It was not an evil thing that pursued them, for its need to kill went far deeper than what we mere mortals define as right and wrong. It was simply a need to be, an urge to sate the growing hunger for flesh. It did not hate them, nor they it, because they knew that it was its instinct to give chase, as much as it was theirs to run.

"The ground beneath its feet stuck to it, keeping it moist and warm; a loud sucking sound accompanying every powerful stride as it broke the twigs that sliced at its prey, its eyes never batting for fear of being prodded. It thought only of the hunt, of the taste of victory.

"The moon overhead and the ground beneath, it chased as they were chased. It ran as they did run. And as it caught them, their flesh biding mercy to its claw, they became one under a common need, a common goal, and came to know and understand each other in the hour of their passing.

"The need to go on.

"In the shadows it caught up with them, and they did not turn away, for they found that they could not bear to fight it any longer, and more than that, did not want to.

"They came to it willingly, tired from the hunt, and felt its tingle wash over their bodies as its breath hit them, and they were surprised at how good it felt. How freeing it was.

"They let the monster take them whole in its passion, biting their lips as they disobeyed all that their parents had instilled in them as children.

"All for that one moment of pure, unrelenting ecstasy.

"Their bodies throbbed and convulsed with pleasure as its tongue draped over them, and from their vantage point, naked and writhing in the shadows, it could see the world of the light out of the corner of their eyes, but the world could not see them, as the darkness sank snugly inside of them.

"And even as it filled them, clouding their thoughts and their actions, their hands going places they were told never to let them go, they could not help but remind themselves how wrong it was.

"That they were bad.

"Suddenly, it began to hurt. Then more and more, until the pleasure was gone, leaving only agony and death that wrenched at their hearts, the darkness enjoying it more and more with every swell of pain that surged through them, barring its massive teeth.

"And when they died it ate them, from the bottom up.

"And all they could think was how bad they were.

"And how much they deserved it.

"And how they could not wait to do it again.

"And how it had all been worth it.

"It came at them from inside the mirror, arms reaching out with tiny mouths at the end of each and every fingertip, devouring them like tiny cannibals, so hungry that they would eat even of their own flesh.

"And when they screamed it was neither piercing nor did it render any help as blood started to pour from their gaping, open wounds, for it was a silent scream, turned inward on themselves. As the scream pierced their very souls, they stopped feeling the thousands of razor sharp teeth, and eventually all they were was the tone of the scream.

"After time, the teeth were always there. The teeth had become a part of them, hard and sharp, covering their exterior so that no one ought see them, and no one would dare touch them for fear that they, too, would be devoured.

"And without the warmth of another the teeth sank deeper and the scream grew louder. It grew until they could no longer even hear it, becoming white noise, and they became deaf to all else.

"So great was their hunger for human contact that they turned on themselves, and became the teeth, both devouring until there was nothing left.

"With nothing left to feed on, the teeth on the tips of the fingers turned to their eyes, gouging them out.

"They heard nothing.

"They saw nothing.

"They felt nothing.

"They were nothing.

"And the teeth on the tips of the fingers went back into the mirror,

"To wait until tomorrow.

"They did not run, for they did not wish to. Instead they stayed there, bathed in light as the darkness swirled around them, taking each breath long and deep, just in case it was their last.

"The beast circled them, clacking its nails against the ground, making them twitch as the suspense rose to a nearly tactile level of unbearableness.

"It was maddening.

"At first, they did nothing. Then, all at once, they turned about and lashed out, pounding their fists into the creature, sending it scampering away, laughing at their attempts.

"That they would try to harm that which they simply did not understand, such being the plight of all mortals.

"But the blow missed, of course, and the arm traveled around the curvature of the earth, picking up speed as it went, until finally, they hit themselves.

"And the blow that would start to harm others

"Would cause their suicide.

"They looked deep inside themselves,

"And they realized that the darkness had been inside of them the entire time,

"Following them like a shadow."

Xander stood on the edge of his bed.

The knife dropped to the floor, tiny droplets of blood spraying off it onto the wall as black ooze took over his body, slithering its way from his veins out into oxygenated air. His eyes turned coal black... then stark red...

... then finally, a sea-green aqua.

He growled, opening his mouth wide.

PREVIEW

GANG WAR

PREVIEW
GANG WAR

Tommy Irons held the knife firmly in his right hand with the blade pressed tight against his left wrist.

The knife belonged to his father. It was a simple hunting knife, its rubber handle wrapped in black grip tape. The faded six-inch blade came up sharp on both sides, without any serrated edges or designs in the metal to make it appear fancy or frightening.

Against his tender, loose flesh, it looked much more impressive than when it rested casually on his father's worktable.

His hair was spiked high, as it usually was, belaying its long length. His heart-shaped face, usually seen with a smile (or at least a grin), was now sewn up in a frown of deep resentment. He wore a stained and tattered white tee shirt under an open blue one. The shirt was denim, like his jeans. He'd fallen in love with that style three years ago after staying up late and watching old teen movies from the nineties and had gone shopping the next weekend. He owned at least a dozen identical pairs.

He sat on the edge of his bed, arms leaned against knees and feet thrown over the side. There were pictures scattered all around of the most recent person to leave him with nothing: Julie Peterson.

His walls were covered in images as well. Pictures that he had taken, pictures that had been taken of him and of his life.

That had always been an annual ritual of Tommy's. Every year, he'd change all of the pictures on his wall to those he'd taken the year before. His father had always called him Shutterbug for it, back when he'd given Tommy's actions any thought.

This year, however, had been different.

This year everyone had started to abandon him, from the beginning of the school semester starting with Jamie Dawkins and continuing through to Julie Peterson. The weeks could almost be marked by a personal loss on his part, either through death or choice or circumstance.

Every time one of them left him, he would turn their picture around. He would never take it down completely, merely flip it so that it faced the wall, sticking a pin in its corners and trying his best to forget the faces contained within them.

Now they were all facing front again. They glared at him again. Judged him again. The eyes that had once seemed warm and inviting now scowled and belittled him.

Jamie, forever frozen, held his cue stick as he awaited Mike to finish his turn. Half cut off by the table, his face was also lost but this time in the shadows of his red Cougars baseball cap. In the darkness, his eyes sparkled from the flash, looking sinister as they stared out at Tommy no matter where he sat in the room.

There were sunspots in Sara's picture, but they worked so well that they enhanced the image. Tommy had zoomed in on her face as she was sipping from the straw of what he thought might have been a Cherry Coke, although the can wasn't visible in the photo. He had framed the shot around her flawless face, accented with wisps of her blonde hair puffing out in stringy wet spikes from each of her black hair bands. Her eyes were wide, showing almost all of her pupils. The girl just didn't seem to believe in blinking, as he used to tell her after examining a roll of film in his darkroom. Now those eyes gawked at him, as if daring him into a staring contest he had no hope of winning even if she wasn't merely an image on glossy photo paper. It was so condescending, the way her eyes seemed to give him the once over, then push any thought of him aside, choosing death over him.

Then there was Derek.

There was no imagination needed to vilify that photo. Staring directly into the lens, arms crossed, eyes squinted and one eyebrow cocked -- he looked ready to leap from the photo and cut Tommy's head off, which he no doubt would have done if given half the chance. Then there was that grin. The sly smile prickling at the sides of his face, the one that he'd always worn. He wore it every day at school, while everyone around him talked about the murders, wondering who would be next and who could do such a thing. He smiled and joked and made light of it every single day... knowing all along that it was him. That he could have stopped and put their fears to rest at any time, but didn't. It was all to impress his father, who spent more time at his job than with his own son. The smile, those eyes... they made you feel like you were being stalked. Like it was only a matter of time, even through the camera's lens.

Then there was Julian Grendel, one of his best friends growing up, sitting back against the couch in his rumpus room, arms stretched out around Cathy and Liz as the both of them leaned in and pretended to give him a kiss on either cheek. His smile was broad. His big blue eyes clearly visible, their color brought out by the sea-green tee shirt he was wearing. He was mocking Tommy, holding out his hands around all that he had and Tommy did not. He was laughing at him, egging him on and yelling at him to do it -- to slice the flesh and let it bleed all over him.

Then there was Randy Owchar, hanging out at The Factory with Justin Langley and Sven Douglas. Never aware that Tommy was taking their picture, they were just loitering by the counter. One of them (Sven, maybe) was holding a Pepsi. As it turned out, all three of them had been Tees, a gang of idealistic thugs that thought way too much of town pride and formed by Randy's mentally disturbed father. Randy had betrayed and hurt them all in many ways, but none more than Tommy.

In the photo each Tee, but especially Randy, was turned away from him. If anything, it was more natural that -- like always -- they didn't give him a second thought. From his place on the bed, Tommy glared up at Randy's face, turned away and sneering at the former friend.

In the background of Randy's picture was Roxanne, the waitress at The Factory. She, at least, was looking directly at the camera. A small grin stretched across her gorgeous face, which was framed by the few scattered wisps of her curly red hair, otherwise drawn up in a bow. She was bringing Randy a Coke, for which he was already reaching into his pocket for change. She, at least, had always been kind to him. She was also one of the women killed by Derek Smith, who explained to a reporter that his reason was to throw the authorities off his trail by killing people outside his circle. Ever since she died, The Factory had not been the same. Joan, the owner, hadn't had any spirit since that day. None of it was fun anymore, instead just a grim reminder of what it had once been, when they had at least been able to cling to the illusion that everything was normal and that they were all friends, despite their differences.

Tommy turned and closed his eyes tightly, batting away a few droplets of tears as he turned to the next picture. His grip relaxed around the knife, then tightened again. He sighed, opened his eyes, and looked straight at the photo of Frederick Windser, who most people just called Sud. The picture was a bust of him, his bald head gleaming under the flourescent lights of the school. He had a fist connecting with the palm of his hand in front of him, wrinkling his dark green sweater at the elbows, distorting the triangles that adorned its chest. He had a vivid, fake grimace on his face as he posed, but the truth of the matter was in his eyes. His eyes sparkled with the mischievousness and playfulness of his true spirit as he posed for his friend's picture. In those eyes were all of the many years of friendship that he had given to Tommy... and the question of why Tommy had betrayed him. It stung more than any photo yet. The night before Sud's death, Tommy had been with his killer. Randy murdered him simply because of his hometown – dead because of a few measly miles -- and the artificial importance of the tags 'Tee' and 'Omega.'

And then there was Mandy.

Amanda Peterson, the light that shone on all their lives, bringing hope to all it touched. She had come to them in their darkest hour, when it seemed like there was no good left in this world, and gave them a glimpse of something better. Her flame burned strong, even as darkness threatened, and maintained her cheerfulness, zest for life and ability to forgive those who had wronged her.

This was part of the reason that Tommy had loved her so much.

In the end it had taken a beating, both physical and spiritual, to finally break her body... but not her spirit. Raped, beaten, tortured, mocked, spat upon... the hope was still in her face, even long after she was dead.

Now, from its perch on his wall, that glow bathed down on him from her pictures on his wall... a mockery of what it had been, for no picture could ever do it justice.

The first was of Cathy, Julie, and Mandy at the Factory. It was one of those spur-of-the-moment pictures that he had taken only because he had his camera on him at the time and they had not noticed that he was standing there until it was too late.

Those were the ones that he liked best. Not the ones where everyone stood in a line like they were getting their driver's license photo, looking stone-loaded out of their minds with red eyes and pasty expressions or had fake smiles plastered over an otherwise dreary expression.

No, he preferred the pictures that were natural. When he could look and remember what people were like, not when they were all dressed up, but every-day normal, in case he ever forgot.

The three of them were sitting on one of the park benches that The Factory owners had bought from the city and fixed up, with an old fashioned street lamp hanging overhead. Where they'd gotten that piece of nostalgia, he'd never know. Never ask, either.

In the picture, Cathy was sipping on her bottle of Cherry Coke via a straw, her head turned slightly. The angle made her hair drape down over a good portion of her face, dividing it into angular lines. She was wearing a tank top with red and black vertical stripes. One of the shoulder straps had fallen over her shoulder, turning the picture from something simple into something sensual.

Julie had actually managed to see him right before he pressed the shutter. She'd been looking past him, at Xander. There was a quirky smirk on her face. When developing the photos and finding he had captured it, Tommy got so happy that he pinned it up while it was still wet, permanently staining the bedspread beneath it with photochemical dots.

And Mandy. She was doing something with her hair. She had both hands up, fixing her pigtails, inadvertently presenting her breasts through the sweater that she almost always wore, or at least some variation of it. There was nothing sexual about the pose, though. It was like looking at a portrait, a painting of a beautiful woman. If done right, there was nothing sexual about the nudity, just beauty. That was the way this was. It was simply her being her, as no other person could, with mouth open to say something to Julie, who was completely oblivious to Mandy's presence.

Tommy had loved that picture for that exact reason. The fact that there she was, being perfect, and nobody was paying attention to her.

Nobody else could see her glow.

Sighing, he turned from the wall to the bed and floor surrounding him.

There were thirty or more photos sprawled out on the floor. Some upside down, some overlapping the others, and none of them in any particular order. There were close shots, wide shots, medium shots, group shots, portrait shots, and the one semi-nude she'd let him do that time they got drunk in Grendel's cabin with Sara. All the shots, no matter their composition, had one thing in common:

They were all of Julie Peterson.

In some she was looking at him, others she was interacting with others. But in all of them, she had cute freckles across the bridge of her nose. She had effervescent green eyes that formed the basis by which every other color in the photos were judged. She had perfectly white teeth, just a little crooked in the front and always in a smile. She had a heart shaped face. She had brown hair with natural light streaks.

In all the photos, she was who she was: never posed and never fake.

One in particular had Julie sitting with Mandy on a bench just outside of school. He told Mandy under false pretenses that he was taking the picture solely of her, so she was posed perfectly, pretending to be a kind of funny-sexy. Julie had been turned toward the smoking section, saying something to Xander when he had called out her name, just before pressing the shutter release button. What resulted was the most natural shot of her possible, from the back wearing a slinky tank top, her head turned over her shoulder to look at him.

He also lingered at the semi-nude shot, in which her shirt was off, revealing a black bra underneath. Nobody in attendance had remembered him taking that picture, including Tommy himself. When he discovered it he had told no one, not even Sud.

Turning away from the pictures, he let a single tear dribble down his cheek as he pressed the knife in; slowly increasing pressure, hissing air as he drew blood, which gradually streamed down his arm.

Pursing his lips, he continued to push, driving deeper into the tender flesh. The pain was overwhelming, shooting in violent bursts between wrist and brain, then everywhere in-between.

Biting his lower lip as the pain got even worse, he held his breath, trying to summon the strength to push down just a little deeper...

His lungs fought back and Tommy heaved a great sigh. He relaxed his grip on the blade and let it fall to the bed. He stood. Cursing softly to himself, he looked around the room at all of the faces staring back at him again.

Sud

Mandy

Julie

Xander

Sud

Randy

Mandy

Cathy

Xander

Sara

Julie

"Argh!" he screamed, eyes bloodshot from pain and rage. He picked up the knife again and sliced it across the wall. Several pictures tore in half, some just below the neckline. Bellowing again, he sliced at the picture of Sud again and again, ripping it up with each strike until it was barely recognizable. He then turned the blade on Sara, and Jamie, and Derek, and Grendel, and Roxanne, and Mandy, and Julie. He tore them all to shreds, sending tiny pieces of photo-paper confetti fluttering in all directions as he waved his arms about wildly with the blade.

He sliced a photo of Xander directly in two vertically, splitting him into halves. He turned to the part of the wall that mainly portrayed Cathy and Mike, grabbing at them with hungry fingers and ripping through the glossy finish on the paper as though it were nothing.

Finally he stopped and looked at what he had done. Sweat poured down his brow and blood down his arm. His breath came in heavy, great gasps.

One photo remained on the wall, hanging from a single tack.

It was the shot of Randy, Sven and Justin, all hanging out at The Factory, awaiting their drinks. Slowly, he reached out with the tip of the blade, gently slicing away Sven and Justin and sending their pieces falling to the floor.

Stepping back and turning away for just a moment, he spun back around quickly and threw the knife as hard as he could at the picture. The knife burrowed a whole two inches into the wall, splitting Randy directly between the eyes.

Tommy stood there, breathing deeply as he squinted at the knife and waited for it to stop vibrating.

ENGEN TIMELINE

With over twenty novels spread over three different series by many different authors, the Engen Universe of titles is growing every day and into genres we couldn't have imagined! From the original ten book *Coral Beach Casefiles* thriller series, its crime novel sequel series *Xander Drew*, our flagship adventure title *Infinity*, or single-novels like *Jacobi Street* or *light | dark,* there's something in the Engen Universe for everyone with more books by more authors on the way soon!

...But how do the events relate to one another, chronologically? While some astute readers have guessed at the potential timeline (some accurately, some not), we're going to finally set the question of the Engen Timeline to rest.

Turn the page for an up-to-date guide of the ever-widening world of Engen, featuring the works of Ellen Curtis, Andrea Hackett, Sarah Thompson, Jay Paulin, and Matthew LeDrew!

In the 10 Years Prior Black September

"Reptilia" by Matthew LeDrew
published in *light|dark*.
Danger descends on a small secluded town in the form of a deadly virus with fantastic and terrible side-effects. Can a small group of doctors escape alive?

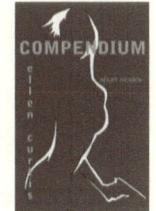

Compendium by Ellen Curtis
Three short stories forming the basis for the Engen Universe's ties to suspense, genetic engeneering, and the supernatural. Features the stories "The Tourniquet Revival," "Falling into Fire" and "At Midnight, the Dawn."

"The Theogony" by Matthew LeDrew
published in *light|dark*.
A tale of young Theo Flaherty of the *Infinity* series and his time admitted against his will to the Black Springs hospital, where he learns to paint, and seeks out his father.

Black September

"Revving Engen" by Matthew LeDrew
published in *light|dark*.
A direct lead-in to both *Infinity* and *Black Womb*, Tasha travels to Coral Beach, Maine on a hot tip about a recently discovered young man with incredible abilities.

Infinity by Ellen Curtis & Matthew LeDrew
Faced with a destiny he's uncertain of, the enigmatic Victor must bring together four unique people with very special abilities… or face the tasks ahead alone. Guaranteed to excite!

Black Womb by Matthew LeDrew
Fifteen years ago, something happened in Coral
Beach, Maine that resulted in the present death of
a seventeen-year-old boy. Now four high-school
students must try to solve the mystery... before
the killer picks them off.

Jacobi Street by Matthew LeDrew
When a mysterious painting shows up at an art
gallery he works at, Bob must work with Eddie
and Sloan to track down its sinister origins and
convince the people living on Jacobi Street of
them, before its too late!

Transformations in Pain by Matthew LeDrew
When two girls are assaulted and one is
hospitalized, the residents of Coral Beach must
put their shared tragedies behind them and stop
the man responsible, as well as unlock the secrets
behind the true nature of the Womb...

Year One: October

Smoke and Mirrors by Matthew LeDrew
The approaching trial of Genblade brings closure
to the people of Coral Beach, until people start
showing up dead in the same manner they did
when he was at large.

"Scarlett" by Andrea Hackett
published in *light | dark*.
Introducing Scarlett, the slightly damaged hunter
on a mission to save others from the monsters
from her past.

"The Inevitable" by Ali House
published in *The Lightbulb Forest*
A young woman must contend with the
emergence of a frightening new power alongside
the emotional high of a first date.

The Tourniquet Reprisal by Curtis & LeDrew
A man lives in Atlanta, Georgia that people
don't talk about, but everyone knows he's there.
He arrived a year ago and turned a gaggle
of uneducated youth into something new,
something to fear.

Roulette by Matthew LeDrew
As the teen suicide rate in Coral Beach starts to
climb astronomically fast, Xander travels to Los
Angeles to fight his most terrifying adversary
yet... and learns that the only thing worse than
looking for release... is finding it.

Year One: November

Exodus of Angels by Curtis & LeDrew
Victor's enigmatic past is illuminated when
Jaycee accompanies him to visit a new friend
in the paliative care ward of the Black Springs
hospital, where Theo also happens to be
searching for a cure for Leigh.

Ghosts of the Past by Matthew LeDrew
Coral Beach faces its most awesome threat when
one of Engen's past mistakes is unleashed upon
the unsuspecting populous. Friends and enemies
unite to fight a common enemy... but will even
that be enough?

Touch Your Nose by Matthew LeDrew
Simon Monk must infiltrate the San Fransico
branch of Shane Industries, a massive company
with deep ties to the Engen Universe. Where do
his true loyalties lie? And can he get out without
causing harm?

Ignorance is Bliss by Matthew LeDrew
After being set through the ringer one too many
times, Xander decides that his life with Julie
needs a little more attention… which is bad news
because a new villain has come to town with his
sights set on Adam Genblade.

"Gristle While You Work" by Jay Paulin
published in *light|dark*.
A short story centering around the rise of a new,
and possibly cannibalistic, serial killer in the
Engen Universe.

Becoming by Matthew LeDrew
For months Xander Drew has been doing his
level best to keep the streets of Coral Beach clean,
which means it's time for the forces of darkness to
strike back… all at once.

Inner Child by Matthew LeDrew
Julie is hospitalized with life-threatening wounds
to both body and soul. But the real threat comes
from the hospital walls themselves, as a demonic
presence makes itself known to Xander and his
friends.

End of Year One

Gang War by Matthew LeDrew
The Tees, a homicidal gang of evil men, has finally been taken down by Xander Drew. But his victory is short lived, as retired Tees are mysteriously killed. With a town of suspects, anyone can be the culprit… including one of their own.

Chains by Matthew LeDrew
Sociopath Derek Smith has been freed from prison and is praying on the weak; and none are weaker than August Styles: a pregnant girl with Down Syndrome who has run away from home.

"Omega" by Ellen Curtis
published in *light | dark*.
A sinister division of Engen begins a series of experiments on pregnant women in a fashion eerily similar to those that created the original Black Womb project.

The Long Road by Matthew LeDrew
Xander meets the American people — and realizes that the world is harsh and wicked, but can also be soft and gentle, even loving. Xander Drew comes of age on the road, and sets his new direction.

Year Two

Cinders by Matthew LeDrew
Detective Horton enters a violent and dangerous world he didn't know existed beneath the veneer of order and structure that he has based his entire deductive method around.

Sinister Intent by Matthew LeDrew
One of the killers Detective Horton could not catch has resurfaced: a serial killer who flaunts his sinister intent in front of the Los Angeles Police Department, making it so that no one is safe.

Faith by Matthew LeDrew
Xander's mysterious and troublesome past returns to haunt him on the streets of Los Angeles; a place where even more people can get caught in the crossfire of the games of death and deceit that makes up his life.

Flickers in the Night by Matthew LeDrew
Lisa Rowdan is hunted by her haunting -- and powerful -- ex-boyfriend Ryan through a lonely city street. Can she escape him?
One of over twenty great sprine-tingling short stories!

Family Values by Matthew LeDrew
Xander and his new friends Crowley, Lisa, and Tim investigate a series of kidnappings and murders that stretch back decades, all of which have the same similar twist: victims being found after years of being missing.

The Future

Fate's Shadow by Matthew LeDrew
When one of Xander's old cases comes up for trial, Megan Greene returns with it. The former friends are led into conflict regarding her client's innocence. However, they put their difference aside when they both become targets of the vigilante known as Shiro Gilbert.

The Future

"Remers" by Sarah Thompson
published in *light|dark*.
In the not-too-distant future of the Engen
Universe, young athletes are the targets of a
scouting program to create the next stage of super
soldier with cybernetic enhancements.

ABOUT THE AUTHOR

Matthew LeDrew holds an Honours Degree in English from the Memorial University of Newfoundland with a minor in Anthropology, and studied Journalism at College of the North Atlantic in Stephenville, Newfoundland. He was honoured to be a jury member of the 2018 NLBA awards.

He has written twenty novels for Engen Books: the ten book *Coral Beach Casefiles* series, *The Long Road, Cinders, Sinister Intent, Faith, Family Values, Jacobi Street, Touch Your Nose, Infinity, The Tourniquet Reprisal, and Exodus of Angels* the latter three of which with co-author Ellen Curtis.

He lives in St. Johns, Newfoundland.